Praise for Ivy Day:

"Ivy Day deftly intertwines the consuming obsessions of fandom and the death-defying allure of celebrity. This charming and surreal fable feels like one of the cult classic movies that it lovingly details."

— Jeff Jackson, author of _Destroy All Monsters_

"Pam Jones's _Ivy Day_ is a quietly creepy meditation on identity as seen through a pop cultural lens rendered nearly mythic. It asks what happens when a society of watchers all put their eyes on one thing, how a society celebrating something for its uniqueness can be slowly covered with a cosmetic homogeneity. Jones does this with distant, nearly hallucinatory prose that still manages to jolt the heart and nerve-endings."

— Andersen Prunty, author of _Neon Dies At Dawn_

"A deconstruction of celebrity—of the ways we hate, love, crave, and fear it—Ivy Day is a novella told with the chilling detachment of a camera eye, unblinking and honest. Stripped of the sentimentality so often associated with the real world's fallen stars, this is a portrait of those who dwell at both ends of fame's microscope; a harrowing literary collage of the relentless, insidious psychopathology at the heart of our celebrity culture."

— Kurt Baumeister, author of _Pax Americana_

"_Ivy Day_ is a novella made of glass and celluloid — positively dazzling, sharp, and so glittery you might not notice how much it's cut into you until you've put it down. While at times reminiscent of Walker Percy or Joan Didion, Pam Jones' characters are existential, mythic, and unequivocally her own. This novella is delicious, brilliant, and disturbing in all the right ways. It will make you remember who or what it is that best feeds the ghost of you, day in and day out, so you can go on living inside your own meat."

— Kailey Tedesco, author of _She Used to be on a Milk Carton_ (April Gloaming Publishing) and _Lizzie, Speak_ (White Stag Publishing)

Also by Pam Jones

Animalia
A Carnival of Birds
The Arizona Room
Anointed
The Joyful Mysteries
Andermatt County: Two Parables

IVY DAY

PAM JONES

SPACEBOY BOOKS

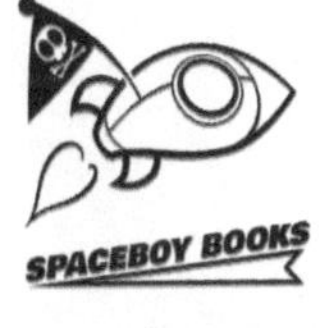

Denver, Colorado

Published in the United States by:
Spaceboy Books LLC
1627 Vine Street
Denver, CO 80206
www.readspaceboy.com

First printed June 2019

ISBN: 978-0-9997862-7-7

To my cousin, Amy Julia Jeuck

Save these organs.
Save this body.
Save your servant.

On Friday nights the Summit Theater had a special. You could buy a ticket to a picture for two dollars, and get extras like pop or sweets or coffee for a dollar each. The catch was that, since everyone and their mother wanted in on the deal, for who knew how many movie houses played up such generosity, you had to get there early. The line began at the box office and wrapped itself around the block.

A bird's eye view gave the queue of moviegoers the look of a centipede, squeezing its segments around a heavy, grey mouse. The public mortuary took up most of the block; JOHN MARK Waterman found himself imagining the assembly of moviegoers quashing the life out of the place, and he tried to lose himself a little more. He doused his fingers with the hand sanitizer he'd brought from home to supplement the morgue's soap. His fingers were ashy from cleanliness and powdery from his diener's gloves, the nails bitten to the quick. When released from his scrubs, his own clothing stuck to him and, reflexively, he took note of each article,

cargo pants, khaki, size M
denim shirt, size M
t-shirt, white, size S
Reebok sneakers, black, size 10

as though he himself were a specimen with effects to be peeled away, collected, and documented.

He swallowed. He popped a piece of gum in his mouth. He exhaled and issued a pink bubble wide as his face, let it hover and touch the tip of his nose, then sucked it back in.

The mortuary released its first shift employees at three o'clock Friday afternoons. JOHN MARK Waterman slipped from his place behind the desk and into his place on the sidewalk, already the eighteenth fellow in line. He did not go home to change or shower, for he rejected all memory, intellectual and sensory, of what he did. He did not fancy a cup of something hot somewhere first. He abandoned any errands that needed running. When it rained, when it snowed, when the summers dragged into their dog days, he took his place in line just as he always had, with a giddiness that began in his gut and spread, like sugar to his blood, to his head, behind his eyes, to the back of his throat, to his palms' wet centers. He did not recall the feelings of heat nor cold nor hunger.

JOHN MARK Waterman went to the movies like a man in love—and, he had to admit it now, that indeed he was.

He had to acknowledge, first and foremost, that Friday afternoons in the movie queue triggered in him a genuine feeling of goodwill toward his fellow man. Not that he ever really spoke to anyone in line, for he would never be one of life's chit-chatters. But somewhere above everyone's heads, running as faintly and as tangibly as electricity, a current of happy times to come connected each person, from the first to the last in line. A communal experience, rejoicing, hallelujah that the week had closed and another, better one may begin, and that no matter what may happen in between, there would always be more days like this.

In his profession, he knew that he ought to be reminded of his own end each day, that it could come at any time, at any place, that the body had ingenious ways of betraying the ghost inside. That morning he had spent washing and readying the remains of a young man, age nineteen, who had slipped in the shower. Had the impact of the tile to his head not got him right away, the running water, in time, would have; JOHN MARK had seen more drowning occur in bathtubs than in rivers. And yet, by the time the young man was washed, restored and preserved as closely as he could be to his living self, JOHN MARK had already seen him turned inside out. The shampoo smell from his last shower had been hosed away and replaced with a pungency that caught you at the back of your throat and under your nose, like vinegar. It made you impersonal, a little disgusted, that someone could be so careless to let themselves go in the shower, of all places. Livor mortis had set in by the time JOHN MARK went to work on him, his bottom half blooming black and violet from his flat rear down his heavily furred legs (which JOHN MARK had taken the liberty to shave after washing him). It might have been the single thing that JOHN MARK shared in common with the young man, and it ought to have made him feel something like humility. Everyone else in his line of work went on about how it made them feel "more in tune" with the heavy truths about life, and got them to "put everything into perspective". JOHN MARK had to admit that he'd been called to this profession for the same reasons.

But he'd been at it for fifteen years, and it made him sick.

He still found it inconceivable that he would be in this place, too, in the next minute, in the next fifteen years.

Jonathan Edwards said, "Unconverted men walk over the pit of hell on a rotten covering."

For didn't everyone know that once the ghost inside was extinguished, all that was left was meat?

It was why JOHN MARK ate kidney beans, mostly, and the occasional egg on toast. The notion of a steak dinner repulsed him; it was what most of the bodies that came in from the county death chamber contained. He'd decided long ago that if he were to somehow, through framing, through bad luck, end up on Death Row, he would order his usual egg on toast, scrambled, and a bowl of kidney beans. Maybe a little tomato sauce to go with it. He would make his last day as much like any other as he could.

That was the thing about the pictures: The star might die any number of ways in twenty different movies, and yet they always came back, pristine and polished, as though resurrected.

The starlet of the day, the one whose name occupied the center of the marquee in the largest block letters available, large enough to be seen from the end of the street, had risen to fame only in the last year.

We've been waiting for you. I've been waiting for you.

When JOHN MARK Waterman came upon this particular interview last night, just casual channel flipping, he had already seen her face and could go no further. She would be tall when she stood up, JOHN MARK could tell that. Weren't all the stars blonde, but her hair was not dyed nor tampered with very much, it seemed. It was the sort of blonde that even naturals tried to emulate, the lightest shade of gold. And there it was, growing from her scalp, as though that were its place of origin. Her eyes were large, the color of them, a mossy green, outshining the whites and starred by her own plentiful lashes— it was this, above all else, that let you remember her humanity. She enunciated her words crisply, without an accent, pronouncing every consonant, her head dipping gently from a long neck when she took questions, her voice low, soft, though it carried far from her chest to where JOHN MARK sat, the sound permanent now in his blood. He could not recall what she was wearing.

In his time as a man who looked upon the faces of other men, alive and then emptied of life, say, at a grandfather and at then his grandson, JOHN MARK noted and filed away the features that came down from one generation to the next; if he were the bragging sort, he would have estimated that he could guess one person's relation to another, to a perfect stranger, from the pattern of freckles, the alignment of the teeth, the set of the jaw, details beyond hair and eye colors. *Seven billion people in the world, wasn't it, and we are all distant cousins.* It was something that nibbled at him as he washed and emptied a body. Another bit was the old scripture, *What has been will be again, what has been done will be done again,* cycling in his brain until his toes curled.

But all things began somewhere, didn't they, before cycling into the next round? JOHN MARK could believe, now that he had seen the starlet's face, that some people simply appeared, without beginning or end. She did not look like anyone he had ever seen, in life nor in its passing.

And he recognized her immediately, as if he had known her always.

The day after he caught the interview on television, he stepped out to the corner store and picked up a magazine, the glossy cover full to bursting with her face. There was an article covering her career on page 67. He stood in the aisle, skimmed the small print, and quickly he absorbed the pieces that everyone would come to know of her: She was ambidextrous. She was a Libra, no date of birth. She had homes in Manhattan and Angels Camp, in Connecticut and New Mexico, where the magazine had photographed her. She posed before an original Georgia O'Keeffe, her head surrounded by the trumpet of a blue morning glory. No exterior shots of the house itself.

"What makes you choose a role?" her interviewer asked. "Where does the attraction lie in your heroines?"

The article described her slow walk from the O'Keeffe to the window opposite, and then her settling into the cushioned seat. JOHN MARK imagined her turning her face to the world beyond, her skin gathering the sunlight. "In her ability to last."

"To last?" JOHN MARK murmured aloud in the corner store aisle.

"To last?" the interviewer had asked in tiny print.

"To go on forever," she continued, "as an example. I don't think people know it, or want to admit it, but a fictional character can be as much of an inspiration to a person as someone in the history books. It's my duty."

The comment, JOHN MARK later discovered, had gathered some ridicule, smeared by journalists and moviegoers for its "inflated air" and being "the kind of bimbo-istic thing you would expect her to say." One critic went on to sourly lament in one of the lesser entertainment magazines, that "...if only she would take a break from her heavy responsibilities and descend from Olympus once in a while, perhaps she might see for herself how little of an inspiration she truly is."

JOHN MARK had not yet seen any of her films. For a brief while, he did not feel that he needed to, for he had already begun the construction of her in his mind's eye of what he understood her to be. More to the point, what he desired her to be, as his private, warmest idea of her that could be tucked away in the recesses of his brain and heart as he removed the still versions of these organs from the bodies that turned up at the morgue. If he went to see one of her pictures, he would have to share her. He would have to share her with a congregation of moviegoers, suffer their whispered comments, their gasps, their coughs, their applause when she vanished at last from the screen and the credits ran and the lights went up. And what of her then? She would be soiled to JOHN MARK Waterman, reduced to the simplest things that everyone, even the meanest idiot, knew about her.

Everyone knew that her name was Ivy Day, for instance.

"But that's not her *real* name, is it?" It was a question he had overheard and finally read in print over the last couple of months, and it repeated itself constantly. This time it had come from the mouth of the woman in front of him, who had loudly been treating her foresight of the picture to the woman in front of her. "I mean, anybody who makes a name for themselves— well, that's just it. They've made a name, made it up. Like, Meryl

Streep isn't really Meryl Streep, for example—" her breath grew thin, her voice high, in the manner of someone exchanging little known, possibly confidential information—"—it's Mary Louise Something-or-other. And Shirley Temple isn't really Shirley Temple—"

This was just the kind of person that kept JOHN MARK away from movie houses. The self-proclaimed "avid moviegoer" or "film buff", who gleaned from esoteric sources Behind the Scenes facts and wry little tidbits about film stars: Judy Garland's pill-popping habits or Rock Hudson's homosexuality. It brought the Olympians back to earth, among the mortal, the fat, the clumsy, the obscure. The gods were human after all, they all but cried. But the thing that really and truly set JOHN MARK ablaze was that people seemed to appreciate this sort of realist approach to moviegoing. The more you knew about the making of a picture was evidence of your enlightened understanding—how much corn syrup made a pint of blood, how the camera had been finagled to make you think that there were two Hayley Millses onscreen when there had only been one.

Don't let them ruin this.

"Her name *is* Shirley Temple." JOHN MARK surprised himself as much as the two women who turned around to find out where that hard little voice was coming from.

"Excuse me?" the woman directly before him asked flatly.

"Shirley Temple never used a stage name." He could not have honestly said whether or not this was true, and his rationale (that distant, underground fire) reminded him that it was an easy enough fact to look up and prove, either way. He had spoken with such confidence that both women were stunned. The woman before him puckered her lips, and then her brow. The woman behind her appeared to smirk, catching the tip of her tongue between her large teeth. JOHN MARK was sure that she was about to inform him that Shirley Temple's name at birth was Shirellanne Platzky, and that her hair was really as straight as bamboo shoots. But when she opened her mouth:

"You know, he's right. She never did change her name." She nodded at him. "It always was Shirley Temple."

And they both took a moment to regard him with such gravity, that he was sure of the rest of the line turning, one by one, to gaze upon him in the manner of disciples in the presence of a prophet. What more would he say? Just one word more, before he rose into the atmosphere?

Of course, the women had turned away before he could blink. But there was this: Although they had already forgotten him in this toe-to-heel procession, the line had begun to move, and he shuffled forward one inch. Time passed, and then another inch. A quarter of an hour limped along, no promises of quickening. The end was not so far away now, though many had been in line long enough to have been slowly consumed by their impatience. A few had gone a little crazy, flapping their arms into the air and stepping out of line. Some were gone for good, hissing that they would find another movie house. A few had only meant to leave just for a moment, however long it took to catch their breath, and threw fits when they were told by their line-mates (and they had really begun to think of everyone as "mates", their buddies in the chain) to "head to the back." No mercy here. Everyone else was in it for the long haul.

JOHN MARK swallowed.

Too often when pieces of his daily routine were beyond his grasp, he fell back on the bizarre, personal rituals that everyone has. Some hum. Some tap a foot, curl their toes, grind their teeth, pull their hair, crack their knuckles, not openly and emphatically, for habits demonstrated in public are always writ small and no one wants to be thought of as the funny one in the flock. JOHN MARK, for example, was wont to nibble at the inside of his cheek. He would swallow the strands of skin that he had managed to tear away and lap at the tiny, bloody hole in his mouth until it healed, when he would begin the process over again. He supposed it caused him some measure of pain, as much as cracking one's knuckles or grinding one's teeth, but he would never have been able to say for sure. Everyone's body was his or her autonomy. Was there any other way to make it through the rough patches, even something as minor as being the tail end of the queue at the supermarket, without going consummately numb? JOHN MARK understood that you had to submit to these little frustrations if you wanted the little prize (if only to reach the end of the line), though you had to remember that your nerves were your own, and not a part of one segment in that long, wormy queue. And so he bit, and often he bled, and often no one noticed, but now and then the cashier would hand him a tissue and it was only when he had left the store that he recognized how deeply he had bitten and how much he had bled.

JOHN MARK swallowed. And he did not bite, not this time, for another inch had passed, and another, and another. Never in his life had a queue progressed so quickly. And never, he noted, had his line-mates (and he really had begun to think of them as "mates") released themselves from themselves and their toe-curling. Everyone enjoyed themselves and one another.

He forewent the candy and soda pop and shunted into the line of abstinent moviegoers. This was where the real schism was, he thought, the sugar people and the ones who could do without. The lobby was packed from wall to wall, but anyone with a bird's eye view of the whole throng would have seen something of JOHN MARK's sentiments: The crowd split once the line had crossed the ticket booth, though the overall congestion made it hard to see, at first. There were so many last-minute hangers-on to the sugar people and to the dry people that they seemed to have formed their own tenacious, albeit temporary knots. Some hovered toward one line and rushed toward the other with little excuses or apologies.

"I had to just grab a drink real quick—I can't get through a picture without at least a Coke or *something...*"

"I'm just going to get a small popcorn this time."

Some abandoned one side altogether.

"Well...screw it. I'm getting nachos."

The movie experience, the sugar people believed, could only be enhanced with the accessories. The M&Ms, the large Coca-Colas that were half and half ice and bubbles, the everlasting strings of strawberry-flavored licorice, the gallon buckets of popcorn that oozed butter through the cardboard. From this came people who purchased collectors' mugs.

And it made JOHN MARK look on with pity. He understood his bias (sugary things had always given him powerful headaches, and soft drinks played havoc with his bladder), but the practicality of it had grown so tenuous within the last five minutes that it had slipped away entirely, and left in its place something that filled him with virtue. He had been right to steer clear of soft drinks and sweetmeats; they softened your mind, which ought to be honed to fine alertness, or how else would you fall into the picture and come out of it remembering, at least, the most important things?

To make his point felt, if not said, he locked eyes with a very big man, who was walking one foot in front of the other to balance a bucket of popcorn atop two boxes of Snow Drop nonpareil candies. JOHN MARK's next step had been to skip his gaze from the man to his sugary burdens and then turn his nose up. He had not counted on the man actually registering *his* disdain, let alone the fact that JOHN MARK Waterman was the only one on his line who noticed the burdens of anyone else. He certainly would never have guessed that the man might approach him, though he would have imagined the weight that the man would carry; JOHN MARK could feel the man's shoes going *boomp boomp* along the floor. In those two steps he was right there, and had at least another foot on little JOHN MARK Waterman. He righted his sweetmeats, squinted, and said, "I hate to bother you, but you wouldn't mind carrying some of this, would you?"

JOHN MARK glanced beyond the big man and tried to make out where his line ended. He could not make out the number of heads for the dark of the hall; this movie house had the idea that they would keep the lights dim outside the theaters, with only the names of the pictures aglow above the doors. If he strained his eyes, he just brought into focus the name of *his* picture: *SS Clelia* and below, *starring Ivy Day.*

He caught the eyes of several people in front of him in the line turning around to watch the exchange with, at first, only foggy curiosity that sharpened when they saw that the big man was working to balance the spilling popcorn under his chin and the little man did nothing but stand and stare like a sleepwalker. Was the little man stupid? JOHN MARK heard them think, or just that rude? He felt himself being slowly squeezed out of this sect. He was at its edge now, and would be officially expelled into the no-man's land between the lines for the sugar people and the ones who did without. He would lose his place. (Really, the people in line were building up behind him, back from the concession with Cokes and treats, and he hadn't moved for maybe a full minute. Of course impatience would grow.)

The woman in front of JOHN MARK, the one who thought that Shirley Temple wasn't Shirley Temple, craned her head around. She looked the popcorn up and down and addressed it. "Do you need a hand? Are you going to *SS Clelia*—"

JOHN MARK put out his own hand. "I was spaced out—so sorry. So sorry—"—he rearranged his face into what he imagined was a cheery and helpful look. He remembered hearing somewhere (from one of his humbled colleagues at the morgue, he bet) that it didn't matter if you had good thoughts, so long as you *did* good things. Eventually, from good deeds would evolve good thoughts. How long did these people really live off the fat of good thoughts before tapping their feet, expectant of reward? Because it was all JOHN MARK could think of. So much for being in love with one and all. He did not see the big man and his popcorn. Far, far down that dark corridor, *SS Clelia* and *Ivy Day* hung in tiny letters just over the big man's head, as if to say, *Here it is. This is how you'll get there.* He'd duck into the theater as soon as they got to the door.

JOHN MARK held out and rounded his arms. The big man blinked, then shrugged. He unloaded the popcorn bucket into those two bowed arms, slipped the boxes of Snow Drops into the breast pockets of his shirt, and threaded the way up the line, down the hall. The man had a foot on everyone, it seemed, and any stragglers out of line jumped back into place when they saw him coming. JOHN MARK, tailing him, buried his face into the odors of butter and salt and something with a tang, cheddar cheese powder. Bliss. He inhaled, just one good huff that would employ both nose and mouth. This way he would get the taste but not the sin; one bite and he would drop his guards and buy out the concession. He saw himself: swiney, going from Crunch bar to gallon pop to trough of popcorn and listening to the picture between munches.

He could not let Ivy Day see him this way.

This was not a strange thought to him, even then. Surely a recording of her would amount as much to having her *right there in the theater.* JOHN MARK had felt her with him from the television the other night. She might have been sitting at the head of his living room.

He huffed again and shut his eyes. If he did not see it, he would not want it as much.

By the time the big man shouldered the theater door open it was standing room only. *SS Clelia* had moved through the gossip vein quicker than a bubble of air, and now the nation was on the brink of collapse if absolutely everyone did not see it. People seemed to know what it was about and how it ended. (Ivy Day, dies—or her character does: A scuba diver, her oxygen supply runs out.) It was not ruined for JOHN MARK. Already the seats were fully accommodated and heads were afloat along the thirty or so rows. JOHN MARK craned his head around. The theater continued to fill steadily, a slow flood, and no one seemed to balk at the idea of having to stand for another two hours, shoulder to shoulder, in the back. A few chanted the chorus to the popular song that had been worked into to the film; it sounded very like "And did those feet in ancient time". Either way, the contagion was in the water, and the tune could soon be heard from the front rows, if not the words.

JOHN MARK caught the tune and hummed it.

Here and there, all down the aisle, he caught her face, Ivy Day's lovely face, appearing and disappearing behind sleeves, hands, other human heads. The expression remained in the same attitude, the eyes trained somewhere above his head.

Damned if it took JOHN MARK Waterman a full minute to realize that people had bought, with their popcorn and candies, *SS Clelia* collectors' mugs, and were sipping from them their soft drinks.

The big man had been clever, JOHN MARK learned, he and his wife having pre-ordered their tickets three weeks ahead of time. "We saw it was going to be a hit," he crowed, "a mile away." He lifted a meaty hand and waved to a smaller, flapping one at the end of the fifth row, in the heart of the theater. Of all places. They waded through the narrow space allotted them by the audience members already seated, now forced to stand at attention to let JOHN MARK and the big man pass. JOHN MARK did not hear himself murmuring, "Excuse me excuse me excuse me" to scowls. Today he met faces as aglow as his own and told them, "Thank you thank you thank you thank you..."

"Well, hi!" The small, flapping hand spread wide for a moment, as though it had become articulate. It was attached to a stringy length of an arm, where bangles clanked, and it was perfectly erect, having spent ages high above its owner's head to signal its meaty mate. "Oh, look at all this! All these goodies, this looks great..." The arm lowered in stages and plunged into the cheddar popcorn. The hand clawed up puffy, orange pawfuls, disappeared, and sprung out again for more. JOHN MARK would never see the body it belonged to. The cardboard bucket that held the popcorn was high, and he was uncomfortable at the thought of asking the big man's stringy armed wife to take it.

The hand waved. "Take my seat," said its voice.

JOHN MARK looked around. Him?

"I'm talking to you," the voice quacked again. "You take my seat. Sitting in the aisle never bothered me."

"It's true," her big husband added. "She camped out for the Beatles when they came to the States."

"Two days—one of them in the rain!—for a ticket," the hand squawked. The fingers nodded nostalgically.

"Worth it?" JOHN MARK asked.

"You bet." The fingers rippled. "I don't think I've been the same since."

"It's where I met my gal," the big man beamed.

"The Fab Four brought us together."

"You bet." The big man, completely softened, did not seem so big anymore. With weird sobriety, he hummed a little of "I Wanna Hold Your Hand".

JOHN MARK scooted, his eyes shut against a perfumed gust, and let the hand (and the woman it belonged to) pass. He got settled in the empty seat. He never relaxed like other people when he sat. Maybe it was a side effect of his trade; even with a dead body, you had to be alert at all times. He arranged himself, back erect, feet flat, as if he expected, at some point, to stand. His hands nested in his lap.

The lights pulsed, dimming, dimming with the noise. The singing took a minute to quiet ("...*did the Countenance Divine shine forth upon our clouded hills...*").

Then dark and hush.

Here was complete silence. No shuffling. No whispers. No light. Nothing to indicate JOHN MARK was not alone and tightly wrapped. It lasted ten seconds, maybe, though he had never been more frightened. He had an idea of where he would one day go. Then the screen flickered with titles, and he could see the faces of the big man on his left, a woman with a messy perm on his right. The tightness eased, for here was company.

And then the screen was filled with a pair of eyes, long lashes, opening, opening. The irises shifted blue, reflecting dark fathoms.

"It's down there." Ivy Day's first words.

And JOHN MARK belonged to her.

How could he describe it?

In two hours when the lights came up, he sat and ruminated, well after the last credit. At once, it was everything he'd wanted and not quite like anything he'd seen.

He might come back to earth if he could remember the plot.

Down there is a bomb. A submarine, the *SS Clelia*, descends into the Atlantic Ocean. Pulses race when the crew and audience learn of the explosive, wormed somehow, in the—what was it? In the submarine's hood, the nozzle. (He hadn't picked up the naval jargon, he was sorry to say.) Ivy Day, a master diver, has the expertise to brave the fathoms *and* to dismantle the bomb. "It might as well be me," she tells her commanding officer, whose persuasions to keep her ashore are brushed aside. The thing of it was that she spoke those words not to her co-actor, but directly into the camera. The screen was full of her, her sadness, her golden reassurance that they, the audience, would be saved. It helped that the theater was so dark. The air grew thin when Ivy Day leapt from the rescue ship and made her descent into chill and shifting black and green.

JOHN MARK chilled.

JOHN MARK filled his lungs to capacity when Ivy Day's oxygen supply grew low, then dwindled to nothing but for what she could inhale in that last breath. Her face looked carved out of ice, not pliable, but peaceful. Her life for the crew, the ransom price and all that. She had saved them. JOHN MARK hoped she knew it, but she'd saved the audience, too.

He could breathe through sobs at her state funeral. In this scene she lies in repose, the camera panning over her casketed body, blanketed in the stars and stripes and then in a layer of flowers. A hero.

And she really looked dead.

And she was going to come back. Praise everything, she was going to come back. And he knew when. Her next film, *Manhattan Project*, was due for release this Christmas.

In his seat, he bowed his head and thought of Ivy Day's countenance divine, superimposed on the shuffling of the other moviegoers getting up and getting out.

He closed his eyes.

When he opened them, the lights were up, the theater empty but for one man. Even the biggest fans had gone home with their collector's mugs. But the two of them remained. JOHN MARK turned around, forgetting his manners to look this fellow up and down. He was all limbs, his arms and legs sparking to stiff, puppet-like life when he stood up. He was one of the ones who stood in the back.

JOHN MARK nodded at him.

The fellow blinked, rippled his long fingers. A closer look revealed that they only appeared longer because of the nails, which were grown out and manicured like a woman's. The nail varnish was flecked silver.

The fellow glanced at his fingertips. "I'm not a secret drag queen, or anything," he said.

JOHN MARK coughed, swallowed. "They're your nails."

"She has a line." The fellow offered it up with steely chill, not defensive. He sounded as though JOHN MARK ought to know what he was talking about.

"How's that?"

"A cosmetics line." The fellow flexed both hands and turned them around, clumsily fanning them out.

"I see." JOHN MARK blinked. "Very fine."

"Yes, sir."

And JOHN MARK Waterman had not lied, for that moment he found himself wondering what his own nails might look like polished and sparkling silver. His eyes strayed to his fingertips, which were very clean, but stubby. It was not an effeminate gesture, he reasoned. Did not the pharaohs of Egypt wear eyeliner? And on the Shakespearean stage, did not the players color their lips and cheeks?

One must look one's best.

It was all for the people.

For if you could not love yourself, how could anyone else love *you*?

At this last thought he had a vision of Ivy Day gazing into a mirror. In his mind's eye, she was genderless, a state of perfection upon which all things male and female could not tarnish. Ivy Day unfurled a tube of lipstick, red as new cherries. She caressed the bow of her mouth with the tip, brought her lips together, blotted gently against the back of her hand to leave a token of self-adoration. And this was not in the least vain. She looked up, into the mirror. "Love yourself," she said.

JOHN MARK didn't know it, but he'd been thinking of the Ivy Day cosmetics ads that ran on the TV. She told the viewing public to love themselves ten times a day.

The fellow with the silver specked was shuffling down his row of seats and striding down the aisle to where JOHN MARK sat. He wore slim, dark-washed jeans and a white, blowzy shirt that reminded JOHN MARK of a caftan. The fellow stooped a little when he rose to shake his hand, which was soft and smelled of lotion, jasmine scented, no sweetness.

In JOHN MARK's mind, Ivy Day brought a sprig of jasmine blooms to her nose. She murmured, "Love yourself." She had a line of skin cream, too.

JOHN MARK said, "You know. That was the first movie I ever saw of hers. I guess I've been missing out on something."

The fellow started, brows furrowing. Then, he nodded, his head bobbing with vigor. "Oh yes, yes, you have," he breathed.

JOHN MARK wanted to ask, for he had never before felt at once humbled, lifted, loved and protected by any one person, if this was what it meant to be—a fan? But the word did not fit. He would not be going home with an Ivy Day collector's mug. What he felt implied something more, a higher plane of devotion than obscene gewgaws. He was ready to prostrate himself at her feet. If she demanded his first-born, he would offer it up to her, without question.

Instead what he asked was, "Is she real?"

The fellow blinked. JOHN MARK might have asked if water was wet. "I have her autograph," the fellow uttered. "And I'll show you."

The thing about starlets is that no one recalls the plots of their films. Ask an Audrey Hepburn devotee to outline the story of *Breakfast at Tiffany's.* Would it be unreasonable to ask a disciple of Marilyn Monroe (since she has decorated her bedroom with the famous still from *The Seven Year Itch,* Marilyn poised over a vent in the street, her white dress rippling like a jellyfish in mid-air) if she can at least tell you the story?

In a nutshell. What is the movie about?

With stars as bright as these, no one can tell you. Perhaps this is for the best, for if there are too many other variables (plot twists, red herrings, allusions) the star herself could not be properly preserved. In all her glory, who would remember her? You can't have too many other things getting in the way. Like Christ to Trinitarians, where the Father and the Son are one and the same, the starlet transcends her character. Audrey *is* Holly Golightly. Holly Golightly *is* Audrey.

Ivy Day is.

This was what JOHN MARK Waterman learned when he followed the man with the painted nails home. They came to a little row of apartments above the Hooray for Hollywood Video, climbing narrow steps and inhaling the take-home popcorn sold below. They blinked when the businesses' neon ad came on in the window, *RENT 2 FILMS for 5 DAYS!* in pink script. It bathed the stairwell and the second floor corridor, and pulsed on and off so that JOHN MARK felt as though he were entering a chamber of the heart.

"You won't have to navigate too much new territory," the man with the painted nails said, unlocking and shouldering the door. "It's only one room."

He felt for the light.

The bulb was weak, and so the room revealed itself in little bursts: An eye, a vast red-lipped grin, white teeth, a hand, one smooth and hairless leg, body parts seizing in and out of the dark until the overhead light settled.

"Oh—" JOHN MARK tried not to squeak.

The man with the painted nails was not sheepish. "I went through all the magazines. But I sent away for photos, too. Signed."

Every inch from floor to ceiling was papered in glossy cutouts, Ivy Day's face appraising them in a million different expressions, sensual, moody, delighted, fierce, rue. Her eyes and hands peered over the tiled space over the sink, she pursed her lips from the corner of the freezer. You could imagine what she must feel at any given moment, as though she were there, a ready reaction for anything you might do. Thinking of jacking off? Behold her smoldering glower from over the mantelpiece (her forehead emblazoned with the word *Vogue*). Thinking good thoughts? Your reward, a redeemer's warm smile from the pantry door and open arms (this was from a fold-out ad for slacks at The Gap). Every so often JOHN MARK could make out pieces of human life: a single bed, a cracked leather sofa, a small television set sitting atop a VCR.

He squeezed himself into the space behind the bed, where the wall had built-in bookcases. The shelves were empty but for one row of videotapes, all of them encased in battered, red plastic. He squinted to read the titles: *Piñata. When You Are Under Glass. Archangel. My Lilac. My Beloved is Mine. Night Shift.* Near the bottom of the videos' spines was printed in much smaller letters, *Hooray for Hollywood Video.* And then, taped in the places where the shelves intersected just above the row of videos, were three headshot photographs, Ivy Day laughing up at him, tossing her hair in this one, glancing behind her shoulder in that, hands flying to her cheeks in the center shot, as though she were ever so happy to run into you, of all people. Each photo bore a sharp signature in silver ink across the bottom. She signed her name the way starlets did, a unique hand, but completely readable. The I in Ivy was the biggest letter, the tails of the Ys in both the first and last names running below Ivy and Day like a watery current.

Here, JOHN MARK grew dubious. He all but mashed his face against the photos. He had to be sure. At first glance, every signature seemed identical. No one signed their name in the same way each time, not even someone who practiced his John Hancock a thousand times a day. The President had a machine that replicated his signature in campaign flyers.

"It's her," the fellow with the painted nails said. "Trust me."

JOHN MARK sniffed and eased himself out from behind the bed. "Where'd you get them?"

"Downstairs. Hooray for Hollywood has a branch of her fan club."

"How d'you know it's really her? Anybody can scrawl on a piece of paper and say—"

The fellow with the painted nails folded his arms, pressed his lips together, glanced at the floor. He had to stoop a little anywhere, even in his own home. It was at this moment that JOHN MARK wondered if his new acquaintance wore Ivy Day's lipstick, too; when the man looked up again, his lips appeared fuller and almost luridly pink.

"It's her," the man repeated, his voice quavering. "Trust me. If this isn't enough, I've got—look—" He shuffled past, making the magazine cuttings rustle and flutter. For a moment, he had to paw along the wall until he uncovered a crack beneath the layers, a closet door so thickly papered that it seemed to JOHN MARK that the man had been swallowed whole by long arms and legs and brilliant smiles.

"I keep these back here," came a voice from behind the limbs. "I don't like bringing them out into direct light too much. I took them with a cheap little camera, so they might fade that much faster—*Shit*—" Something crashed to the floor—"—but this is only a little of what I've got. Hooray for Hollywood, as it happens, runs the local chapter of her fan club. We've got items you wouldn't believe—"

In all the time his host had been in the closet, JOHN MARK had been reading in a fuzzy half-daze the captions of the ads for Ivy Day Cosmetics. *Love yourself* scrolled beneath her lip-printed hand. *Love is patient* unfurled hazily above Ivy Day's brow, the eyes made wide and bright by the kohl. He never once found it odd that an actress—a performer—should carry a line of makeup. Musicians had their names on perfumes—would you smell like Madonna if you wore her scent? Did she smell of oranges and cloves in real life? Would you love yourself and, consequently, would the world love you if you painted your lips with Ivy Day gloss? It did not seem impossible. Nor did it seem unusual for a man to paint his own face—for what wouldn't you do to make the world love you?

As JOHN MARK drew closer, he saw that not every cutting on the wall was a picture, and not every picture was part of an ad. Some were articles, scissored from gossip magazines and taped together with their respective photos of Ivy Day's alleged residences. Unlike most starlets, Ivy Day's homes were not sprawling, grand affairs, tacky with columns and gold leaf and animal topiary. Her tastes were simple, small, all angles and natural elements, stone and wood and iron, very Frank Lloyd Wright. Or her houses were part of the scenery itself, an earth ship cut into a hillside in New Mexico, a geodesic dome rising a little below the tree line in California.

The caption for each of these articles begged the question, *WHERE IS SHE?* It was unlike other celebrities, who had to leave their sacred spaces to do ordinary things, shop, go to the dentist, have their dogs groomed, you could keep a tab on where they were at any given time, based on their comings and goings. Someone saw Katharine Hepburn at the Stop & Shop, she must be at her Connecticut home—that kind of thing.

Ivy Day never left.

Or was never there.

Instead of *WHERE IS SHE,* this raised in JOHN MARK's mind other questions. What did she eat, if she never left/was never there? Did she need to eat? Did she sleep? Was she as curious about her fans as they were about her? Did she watch them with (if not identical, then comparable) devotion?

It did not seem unlikely that she knew where JOHN MARK was at this moment, even if he could not see her.

Her eyes were not blue, but green. For a moment it stood out, the color of bluegrass, to bathe the room. And then it receded.

"Now," the fellow said, very close behind and right in JOHN MARK's ear. "Here's something you *must* see."

A photo, stark, bright lights illuminating the edges of a steel tabletop. And upon it, Ivy Day.

"Asleep?" JOHN MARK asked, though he knew this to be untrue. Impossible. She must have been going blue as the camera flashed.

"It's your line of work," the fellow coughed, impatient. "What do you think?"

"She's not—"

"She is. There." The fellow put a funny emphasis on the word There, as though he were trying to work in the word Then. As in, something that had happened Back Then, when the photo was taken.

She was dead Then.

She was dead There, but not anymore?

Explain.

The fellow did. "You know how in the movies, the big action-packed flicks, when an actor gets shot or keels over after being poisoned or something?"

JOHN MARK thought. Mick Jagger was hanged at the end of *Ned Kelly*, and he came back. Vincent D'Onofrio shot himself with an M14 rifle in *Full Metal Jacket*, and he came back. These things were true, there were more movies to be made, after all. People counted on them. JOHN MARK had reconstructed (to the best of his ability) the skull of a man, age sixty-seven, who had blown his brains out with a pistol; half of his face caved in, gritty around the edges, looking for all the world like an old melon. This man did not come back.

Some of us have to come back, JOHN MARK thought. Some of us have to come back so that we may all live—in something.

The fellow lurched behind him, dragging a beanbag chair. He plopped into it. "You're not supposed to have favorites," he said sheepishly. "But I could watch *My Lilac* over and over. You?"

JOHN MARK straightened. His voice was crisp, bold. "I have no favorite." This was untrue, but he had no room left for doubt. His love was immediate and consummate.

The fellow blinked, tried a little chuckle, silenced when he saw that JOHN MARK was made of stone. "Well. All right. I guess you won't mind *My Lilac*, in that case."

JOHN MARK bathed in the screen, heedless to the movie itself. He'd reasoned now that the small words and frippery did not matter so much as the star who carried it all. Ivy Day died at the end, that much he grasped. But she would come back. Forever and ever, she would come back.

Beside him, the fellow said, "I thought you said you'd seen this before."

Ivy Day. That was all.

There were three girls who wanted to look like her.

They were freshman, fresh faced. They stood in the hair color aisle of the supermarket. They carried a basket, already half-full, of lipsticks ranging from burgundy to coral, liners, foundations, kohl, powders, potions, pomades. They would contour, carve, create the balance of the world in their faces.

They split and regathered. They held samples to each other's manes, compared complexions. Then, clandestine, they smuggled their loot beneath their jackets, crept away. It was not so much that they didn't have money, as they didn't want anyone to know how badly they needed the face paint.

Ivy Day.

How many people looked like her?

They were Angie, Becky, Crystal. They wanted to be Adrienne, Brooke, Celesta.

Celesta had her own bathroom, so everyone went to her house.

They unloaded their loot on her bedspread, genuflected before the vanity mirror. Celesta was one for taste, and so her bedroom walls were free of the usual magazine dissections. Instead, in accordance with an article she'd read that covered the décor of celebrity homes, one corner of the room was painted cream, the other colored, one wall apricot and the other Persian green. Her bedframe was gilt, her wardrobe hanging on rolling racks, her necklaces draped from the edges of the mirror. This was her sanctuary, and the guiding place for those who followed her. Celesta was destined for great things; if nothing else, her bedroom was testament to that, and having taste was half the battle.

You led by example and others followed. First, they wanted to be like you. How long before they would want to become you?

"Blonde." Brooke read the word from the package. The others nodded. Brooke brightened the lights wreathing the vanity mirror and held the sample envelope next to her face. She was already blonde herself, dour, ashy strands that thinned to the witchy ends. She was trying to grow it out, but somewhere around her bust it always took on the appearance of an old wig. She touched the ends to the envelope, the flap of which was colored a shimmery gold.

Adrienne stepped in. Her own hair was carroty, intermittently streaked with the shade she wanted from top to bottom. You could only see it in certain lights. When she angled her head back, so far back that it looked as though her neck had been broken, the right color lit her head from behind, and the edges became a crown. She stood this way at the mirror before the strain (and the silliness of this posture) called her to right herself.

Celeste looked perfect. She and the envelope were a match, and no eyes could be deceived. She provided the bathroom, the privacy. She gave herself a quick appraisal in the glass (bit her lips, wiped her teeth) and pulled on the rubber kitchen gloves. Adrienne and Brooke jumped at the squeak they made as they slid over her fingers.

Adrienne asked, "Have you ever done this before?"

Brooke said, "Sure she has. Obviously. Look at her."

Celeste frowned. The elastic snapped against her wrist. "What's that supposed to mean?" She shook her hair back from her ears.

Brooke realized her misstep and examined the tabletop clutter.

Adrienne, obedient, scoffed. Then, she dropped to one knee to go through her purse; it was more of a satchel, red pleather and wide-mouthed, big enough to fit a pair of shoes, a change of clothes. She brought out a magazine. "God," she breathed, as though she beheld the deity in its pages. "Just like that." And she splayed the magazine for them. *IVY'S DAY COMETH AS A THIEF IN THE NIGHT.* And below the article's title, in smaller letters, *Is there a new film in the works for Ivy Day?*

There, filling two pages, Day's dear face.

It was tacky, but Adrienne planned to save the article so that she could paste the cuttings to her bedroom wall. They loomed at her bedside, her icons: There was Selena Quintanilla and Princess Di, Marilyn Monroe patting down her billowing skirt. Beside her was a clipping of Jeff Buckley's shaggy head, a halo of hearts around. The Beatles, Kurt Cobain. A pigtailed Judy

Garland as Dorothy Gale. Adrienne loved them. They smiled her to sleep.

Celeste gave them a look, but she never said anything about them.

The girls moved, clustered, into the bathroom, led by Celeste, who turned on the cold water in the bathtub. Brooke and Adrienne knelt and allowed her, the true blonde, to bury their heads in foam. The room smelled of jasmine. The girls, all three, bit their lips against the water's chill, rushed for the towels as soon as the first stage of this transformation was done.

Turbaned, they returned to the bedroom to sit, cross-legged, in the middle of the rug. Celeste, warming her hands between her thighs, told her friends that it was important to let their hair dry naturally. Adrienne and Brooke nodded, and their heads sunk a little beneath the towels' weight; they dared not question her.

To kill time, they practiced posture. Celeste put on a tape, Saint Etienne, full of sparks and gold, and they straightened their shoulders and walked the length of the bedroom, hips first. They caught themselves in the mirror, only a wisp of what they were, a flash of hair, a lanky arm, and they fell in love with themselves. For here was the divinity in them, after all. All they had to do was coax it to the surface.

The tape deck sang, a cover of Neil Young's dirge. Unlike Young's funerary wail, this bounced the words up and down. Still a warning, but you would never know it. The girls broke their march to dip and groove. *Only love can break your heart, only love can break your heart, only love can break your heart.*

And that was the thing about loving yourself: You could never disappoint. You couldn't afford to, and so you could always be relied upon to improve. You did have to live with yourself.

Brooke ripped the towel from her hair and twirled it above her head like a lasso. She looked to Celeste and said, "I'm ready."

Brooke's hair was thin and dried quickly. She would have to be patient for Adrienne.

Celeste thought they might use this time to paint themselves. She began on her eyes. None of them had really worn makeup, save for smears of lip gloss now and then. And then, this year, crystallized in its urgency, it was all they could think of. They scoured magazines and hoarded samples. They pilfered mascara wands from their mothers. They were secretive in their rituals, experimental and pushing the ever-shifting boundaries of decency. If someone came to the door, and there they were, mid-stroke, half-painted, the girls crammed their treasures away, bleating, "Don't come in, don't come in—" Moms grew suspicious; was it drug use or group masturbation?

If anything, they had formed a cult of their own, burning and glittering and all for them. None of this mother-daughter bonding whatnot.

Celeste blinked and she felt the weight of her thickened lashes. A little itch, but that was no bother.

She turned to Adrienne. "All right," she said. She went to loosen the girl's hair from the towel, which, in their dancing, had drooped down her back in the manner of a veil. Adrienne shook her hair out; it was still a bit damp, if only just this side of it. Celeste tried to persuade her to let it dry a few minutes more. Adrienne would have none of it, so keyed up she was to begin the transformation. She turned to look at the magazine, splayed upon the bed. She put her finger to Ivy Day's hair and groaned.

"It's dry enough!" she cried, and she whipped her own hair around and around her head. Celeste and Brooke shielded themselves against the wind of it.

"Fine, fine," Celeste muttered. "It's dry enough. Let's go."

Back to the bathroom, where Adrienne and Brooke knelt once again over the tub. This time, their hair hung, combed and lapping over their heads. Their hands were folded between their thighs, their eyes closed, at peace.

Celeste read the instructions on the back of the box three times, to make sure all understood what was to happen. "It might sting, it says," she noted. "You're sure?"

They nodded, their faces veiled.

"Okay." Celeste filled her lungs and filled a kitchen spoon with the sour-smelling stuff from the envelopes in the box. Even as she read the instructions (a fourth time to herself, muttering as she would an incantation), she was sure in her gut that there was something that had slipped, reading too fast or too slow, a missed word, something small that would lead to something hideous. She made sure that the box said a tablespoon in a five-ounce bottle of clean water. She couldn't find the tablespoon. She couldn't find the five-ounce nozzled bottle her mother used to touch up her own roots. She made do with the kitchen spoon and an old baby bottle. They were about the same. Approximations, reinterpretations.

She made an excuse to go into the bedroom and looked to the photo in the magazine. Ivy Day looked up at her, golden hair a crown; she did not smile, but her eyes were warm and Celeste felt that the starlet had found her, touched her, inspirited her.

It would be all right. It would hurt, but it would be all right.

Calmed, Celeste went back to the bathroom. Adrienne and Brooke were where she'd left them, still bent over the tub. She grabbed the three-ounce baby bottle and shook it. She stood behind Adrienne, who palpitated so much her teeth chattered. Without waiting for her to brace herself, Celeste poised the bottle over her hair and squeezed. Neither she nor Brooke flinched when Adrienne unleashed shriek upon shriek. All kept their eyes closed; it sounded horrible enough, miraculous enough, without having to look.

Transformations are never easy. Breast buds hurt when they blossom. Menstruation kills. Erections creep up and overtake you. It was worth it in the end, wasn't it? Pain is beauty, all that?

Tribulation worketh patience. It was something Ivy Day had said in one of her movies. She had played a nun in the French Resistance. She'd worn a veil for most of the picture, but this was the scene in which she took it off, revealing wafts of golden tresses, cut short, but beautiful. She died at the end, shot through the heart by a German.

Remembering that made Celeste squirm with contempt, now more than ever, as she doused Brooke's scalp. Brooke did not scream like Adrienne, she whimpered. Celeste wanted to slap them both; if Ivy Day suffered without noise, what was their excuse?

"Stop it," Celeste muttered.

"It hurts—" Brooke whined, let the drawn-out sound break into sobs. "It really, really hurts—"

Adrienne had quieted and was gathering her breath and releasing it in short, halting hisses. "Think about something else," she gasped. "Think about how great you'll look. When it's all done, think about how great you'll look." Neither she nor the others could say how great she looked, for none of them dared to open their eyes. Adrienne never would have admitted that the alcohol, or whatever it was, in the hair coloring did not sting but burn, and that behind her lids she had visions of sores that oozed over her scalp. Celeste imagined from the screams that this may very well be true.

And now, here was Brooke, who bawled, "I can't."

Celeste said, "Yes, you can."

"No, no, no, it hurts too much—"

"Yes, you *can.*"

"Please, just turn on the water. Just turn on the water."

Adrienne hissed, "You have to leave it in for twenty minutes."

Brooke wept. "How long has it been?"

Adrienne filled her lungs and her voice was tight. "Ten more minutes. You'll be fine."

Meanwhile, Celeste's eyes itched. Since Adrienne calmed down, she'd had time to notice. Nothing hurt, it crept up on her, made her eyes water. She rubbed the corners with her pinkies.

Brooke was trying Adrienne's breathing technique, but her breath came too quickly. "Please, turn on the water."

Celeste said, "Two more minutes." She had opened her eyes long enough to check the timer. "If we run your head under the faucet, it'll all wash out."

Brooke seemed to quiet at this. She held her breath and emptied her lungs, she was suspended in these last moments, when the sting of it seemed to have reached its peak, where pain excels to something close to pleasure. She moaned, but her tone had changed, as though she were beginning to like it.

The timer went off.

The girls, all three, opened their eyes.

They gathered at the mirror over the sink.

"God," Brooke breathed.

The dye had worked. They were true blondes.

They stood gobbling for a minute, when Adrienne rubbed the corner of her eye and Brooke did, too. "It's not like an eyelash," Adrienne grunted, "but it feels like the whole eye*ball* is what itches. Do you know what I mean?"

Brooke nodded, made the brave move of going in to scratch the red in the far corner. "Well," she sighed, "at least the mascara doesn't come off. You could probably go swimming in this stuff and it'd stay on."

And she was right. No matter how often the girls rubbed or scratched or wept, their eyes remained large and thickly furred. No grime, no slime.

Celeste balled her hands in her pockets. She would not scratch, not for anything. A little itch, but that was no bother.

She blinked and told the girls to follow her into the bedroom. "I read you're supposed to cut it right after bleaching."

JOHN MARK had a routine. He would work his hours at the morgue. He would go home and wash. He would stand on line at the Summit for *SS Clelia*, and then for Ivy Day's next film, an adaptation of *The Dybbuk*.

There was quite a crowd, those who were the moviegoers and those who stood in the street in protest. Ivy Day's presence in this picture had caused a bit of controversy; those who stood in the street spat at her blonde hair. She did not look the part. She was "a prime example of what whitewashing is all about".

Those who stood in the street had failed their purpose, however. Their presence was not a deterrence, but a bit of free advertising. The more they shouted, the more they spat, the longer the line of moviegoers got. People were curious. People were seduced. Forbidden fruit has that effect.

The people on the street hissed. "Whitewashed."

"The status quo."

"You can just keep the system going, just keep the old system going."

"It's people like you who keep blonde hair and blue eyes where they don't belong."

JOHN MARK wanted to shout at them, *Her eyes are green.* But he looked ahead, and moved with the line.

He'd taken the leap and joined her fan club. In earlier days, he'd sworn that he would never in his life sink that low, but, as though guided by his ghostly faculties, he found himself sitting in the back room of Hooray for Hollywood Video, one out of an entire congregation that worshipped the same god. They sat on metal folding chairs. They sipped coffee. There was a collapsible table where a potluck was arranged, of store bought cupcakes, trays of crudité and dip, chips and salsa, lemonade in Dixie cups. JOHN MARK did not flinch when one of the club members sidled up to him and, without waiting for a Yes or a No, proceeded to paint his nails with Ivy Day's signature polish. They compared colors and palettes and daubed one another's faces with all the cosmetics the Ivy Day line had to offer. JOHN MARK would never learn anyone's names, but he did learn how to bake his face. In a few weeks, he would perfect the nuances of clown contouring, streaks of pastels across his cheekbones and down his nose.

When he looked at himself in a compact mirror, he could not breathe. "Oh," he whispered. He was gorgeous, as close to being sculpted in Ivy Day's image as he could be.

Like the package said, at last, he loved himself.

Everyone in the club seemed to have an esoteric tidbit about their idol to share, a photograph, a token.

Ivy Day was not her name. This they all agreed on.

Her name was Senna van der Pool and she was born in Argentina.

Her name was Leona Flowers and her first language was Portuguese.

She was a vegetarian.

Her favorite food was steak tartare.

She was brought up in a convent.

She was brought up in an orphanage.

She was born to a family so wealthy, they could afford to keep their names out of the press.

Here was a picture of her as an infant, her first Halloween, costumed as a red crayon.

Here was a newspaper clipping from Himmel Creek, Texas, an honor roll listing for the junior high school. A name was highlighted in pink, *Fern Guilfoyle.*

Here was an ad torn from a magazine, a model long and sleek in jeans and a white, cropped t-shirt with long sleeves. She, too, was blonde and had a golden something about her, that aura that made you want to look at her over the clothes. But she could have been anyone. The club member who passed around the ad was certain that this was Ivy Day in her days before stardom.

What kept them all going, like the circulation of blood, were not the things they knew about her, not what she was, but what she could be made into. Ivy Day coveted her privacy. She appeared when she wanted to, where she wanted to. That much of her they knew.

And it was all well and good, JOHN MARK thought, until an image of Ivy Day swam into his mind. It was so unsavory he very nearly blotted it out before he was conscious of it. But he was not quick enough. He imagined Ivy Day answering the call of nature, squatting in a public restroom. She was in sight, sound, smell of everyone around her. He wobbled his head, erasing the blasphemy. Maybe it was the vegetable tray that got him; broccoli carried a stink when it was left out. He closed his eyes and found himself there again in that public restroom, where Ivy Day emptied her bowels into the same pit as her disciples. The cubicle was scarred and inked in all four corners by previous occupants. *K was here. Barb shat here.* And here was Ivy Day, the golden girl, carving her initials with one manicured fingernail.

He pulled out and opened his eyes to the back room of Hooray for Hollywood, and he stood. He excused himself, sounding pinched, for suddenly he felt that if he spent another minute among these people, these pretenders, he'd become dirtied himself.

This was how gods died. They were pulled to the level of men. First, they thought as you did about little things, in spite of all that rot about working in mysterious ways. Then, they had husbands and wives. Then, they ate, when a god, if he were truly omnipotent, shouldn't need sustenance of any kind. And if they ate, they had to excrete. And then where would the difference lie between the men and the gods?

It made JOHN MARK sick.

On the way out, he helped himself to one of the new releases, Ivy Day in *Portals*, and a few old favorites. Ivy Day as Ophelia, Ivy Day as La Esmeralda, Ivy Day as Sister Suzanne Simonin. Drowned, hanged, diseased, she died and was resurrected every time. Tragedy and glory. Gore and gold.

JOHN MARK could never say what it was that brought him back to her, film after film after film. He was devoted. He'd even begun to collect images of her, gleaned from magazines, postcards, newspapers, pasting them all up and down his apartment until it looked like the lair of a teenaged girl. He would never have admitted that his place was beginning to look like that of the fellow's he'd met that night at the Summit.

Isn't that the way of worship? whispered a small voice in the back of his head. *The way you do it is the right way. And no one does it the way you do it, because no one can. Not really. Because your way is the best way. The only way.*

He popped one of the videos into the VCR. He didn't care which one.

JOHN MARK sat inches before the screen, his shoulders humped, nude but for the blanket he'd taken from the couch and swaddled himself in. He kept one eye on the television, the other on the toenail he was painting, Ivy Day's peony pink.

She had a way of looking at the camera as though she were looking at you. JOHN MARK would not hear of it any other way. She was looking at him, in his sloppiness, and she loved him for it, because he would die and she would not. He was how she lived, how she ate and breathed. He, and others like him, were how she thrived.

He finished his toes and started on his fingernails. He mouthed the lines she delivered; he did not understand the words so much as the cadence. Anybody could say, *You'll be there, and I'll be here. The way we're supposed to be.* Ivy Day could carry the film with that line; an article in *Variety* reviewing *Portals* opened with it.

The scene: Ivy Day's character was a woman who communicated with her husband telepathically. They were torn at first by war, and then, suddenly, a wormhole, bringing the husband to another universe, leaving Ivy Day in the known world. They hear of a rift in the Cloisters Museum. (Admittedly, there was a lot about this movie that lost JOHN MARK. He resolved to pay better attention the next time he watched it.) And then comes last message the husband receives before she falls into the rift. *You'll be there, and I'll be here. The way we're supposed to be.*

It could have been cheesy.

It could have been crap.

It had all the elements of bombing, so the magazines had said.

As it was, the line popped up in articles. It was carved onto jewelry. It was printed on postcards. People wove it into their wedding vows. It was a meme. *Portals* was generating Oscar buzz. "I think we can just mail Ivy Day the award now," a TV commentator had quipped. "Just get that part of the ceremony over with."

You'll be there, and I'll be here. The way we're supposed to be.

She was looking at him. She was speaking to him.

She was looking at the ceiling. She was speaking to the surgeon.

Ivy Day had come out of a long sleep, from a dream in which someone had called her Mary. She'd had dreams like this before: She was always younger, in a yard with a pool. Someone, a woman, called from the ether above. The name shifted. Today it was Mary, the last one it was Sylvie.

She spoke to the surgeon in single words, the ones he instructed her to say. "Starlight. Jam jar. Zests. Guanajuato." Her speech was intact. Next, he asked her to move her fingers, and then her toes. She made a folded cavern with her hands, her forefingers for the steeple.

She had died, or something this side of it. The last time, they had shot her through, once in the hip, once in the shoulder. Wasn't that how a singer had died? Selena Quintanilla, beloved chanteuse of the Tejano scene, shot by a fan. That was what Ivy Day had heard, anyway.

And now there was today.

And look at her now.

Look at her, Ivy Day, now.

It had been so all-encroaching, so golden, that she could not recall the point at which she had begun.

What was her first picture?

Who had discovered her?

She ought to remember those things. As it was, as she stood, it was as though she had always been, like a god—she had made herself, never having been birthed.

The surgeon, after every procedure, presented her with a full-length mirror, to make sure that his work was to her liking. This time, she had sustained abrasions and breaks, splinterings, what you might expect if you were thrown from a cliff. They'd had to patch her up. It was how she came to know these operations, "patchings up". The discs of her spine are alternating pieces of steel. Her femurs are held together with pins. Beneath the filaments of blonde gossamer, the trademarked tresses that garnered their own shade, Ivy Blonde, were plates that kept her skull from leaking what was perhaps the only organism left to her body. Even then, her memories of the life before had a gauzy texture. The only way to solidness seemed forward.

And she raised herself from the gurney. The doctors shifted back, their slippers making whispers across the floor. In the mirror, you would never have guessed at the butchering that had to be done to rebuild this creature. She could not have said what left of her was decomposable. Even bits of her skin were plastic. Everyone guessed, but no one said, that Ivy Day could live for a thousand years.

She turned to the surgeon. He was trembling, exhausted, barely keeping his old eyes open. His hands were still. He was the best. He cut into the best. He made stitches seamless and supplemented bones with the stuff of Titans. He turned back the clock for aging faces. Ivy Day had hired him as her personal surgeon last year, and the public was in an uproar about it for a minute or so. But then, they saw her movie, and they had nothing but glowing things to say about her.

"You," she pronounced, "are a genius."

The surgeon flushed under his mask.

In her latest picture, she was a vestal virgin, a convicted murderess of a Roman Senator. She did not want to tell the scriptwriter that vestal virgins were executed by premature burial, not flung from the Tarpeian Rock. Imagine the plunge, the sudden lurch into nothing, and unaware of the crash at the bottom of the pit. Everyone above quiet that first day—and then after, it would be all they could talk about. It was the perfect way to die, she thought.

And so, that was what had happened. Ivy Day had been thrown from a cliff, ten cameras recording the whole thing, and she had risen again, to as much adoration as before.

The papers said she performed her own stunts. This was something that always threw people. Stunt people, though brave, did not die, did not go out and give themselves to the lions in the pit. They teased them, maybe stuck a hand through the bars and snatched it back in time.

Because they had to, her doctors had pronounced her dead, as a result of her stunt work, on seventy-two occasions.

She'd tried to explain it to someone not long ago. It had been at a television interview, an artists' round table discussion. Sting was there. Andy Warhol was there, Joan Didion and Sun Ra. They'd been talking about their immortality. There were lines she'd come across that wound what all she'd been feeling into something that made sense. *One must discontinue being feasted upon when one tasteth best: that is known by those who want to be long loved.*

"*So teacheth Zarathustra,*" Sun Ra had added.

"Neat," Andy Warhol had murmured.

She could not have been the only one in the world who knew this. Anyone who wanted permanence in the people's history knew that there was a right time to go. Selena was at the height of her fame. Princess Diana was photographed up until the end. Now they were preserved, as if in crystal. As many times as Ivy Day had reached the end, she had always been brought back. Someday, the blackness would have to go on and on. Only then, would she become immortal. A piece of her would be, anyway.

Another picture, another stunt. It all moved so quickly, she couldn't recall the moment at which she was felled. In this one, she was a deep-sea diver, a hunter of pearls. It was a heated pool, but deep. She had come up too soon.

When she woke, she was on the gurney.

Here was the surgeon, and there were the doctors.

Was this the seventy-eighth time she'd died?

Maybe, at last, the hundredth?

They cut into her brain and Ivy Day went under again.

She felt herself falling away, much in the way she had on the day of the shoot off the (reconstructed) Tarpeian Rock. For a moment, it was as though she had broken the barrier of what the future was supposed to be and come through to THE END.

THE END, and that ought to be it.

There was blackness, yes, but it was finite.

She had said to herself that the only direction she moved in was forward, but it was during these periods of falling away that she entered another universe, one in which she was small and stood in a yard with a pool. And someone called her Mary, or Sylvie.

There were other places, too, other situations.

Sometimes, she was gangly, maybe eighteen or so, lying on her back in a cemetery, broad daylight, beneath a headstone that read, *Precious in the sight of the LORD is the death of His saints.* There had been a boy with her, gangly, too, but golden-skinned and green-eyed. He was on top of her, his face in her neck. Her hands were across his back. A beetle crept up her knee. She could not breathe, though it was not out of fear. This was a joy she'd wanted to savor so badly she took it in sips. And nearly went under.

Sometimes, that same boy was leaving her. She was in class, at school. Sometimes, the teacher was reading poetry at them, *Shall I compare thee to a summer's day.* Sometimes, it was a lecture on the Fall of Rome. Either way, the note was the same: *This is too much.* That was an agony, all right, like being run through with an icepick. She knew that she would feel lobotomized for a while after that; first love, first loss, that's how it was supposed to feel.

Other times, she was saying yes to him. They were walking on a trail, green-wooded, salt air, a day in March. He got down on one knee. She wept and wore his ring, a Claddagh made of sterling silver. Had this been before or after the note? Had she been the one, in the end, to leave him? Had she been the one who'd said, *This is too much?* Whatever became of the Claddagh?

Sometimes, as right now, she was Mary. Whoever was calling her was clearer now, saying, *Mary, Maaa-reee,* in a sing-song. There was the pool; that was clearer, too. It was above-ground, shaped like a bowl, full of icy water. The lawn was hot, wet. The house behind her did not impose, not like the ones Ivy Day lived in now. Was that her mother who called her?

When Ivy Day woke, these pieces sunk back into the ether. They were real enough, in the way that dreams are real, or maybe, more to the point, in the way that someone else's life is real to you.

She brought it up with her analyst, who said, "It's what makes you a great actress. It's what makes your work tangible. I can't stress enough the importance of listening to one's dreams. Only now, people are just realizing that. Jung was right all along."

But that wasn't it. Ivy Day said this from the chaise lounge in the library of her New Mexico desert home. Her analyst knew she was there, but the rest of the public did not.

"All right," the analyst said. "Memories, then?"

And, after Ivy Day thought about it, that wasn't it, either. Not quite, for some of them did not always ring true. The pool, the yard, the voice from above calling her Mary. The boy seemed real, she could believe that had happened to her, at some point—before she was Ivy Day.

The analyst hummed, sat forward in her chair. "Envy, could it be?" She sounded inspired. "Envy of the old anonymity? Being able to melt into the universal experiences that the rest of us have? Being small, impotent, living modestly, answering to someone—the mother figure?"

No. That was certainly not it.

The analyst asked, "What do you feel in this memory, dream, whatever you'd like to call it? Do you feel safe?"

No.

"Maybe I ought to rephrase that. Do you feel taken care of?"

Yes.

"But not cherished?" The analyst charged heavily, and she was good. Ivy Day hoped that she was discreet. "This memory, or dream. On the surface, it sounds very safe. Idyllic, really. A summer day, blue skies, green lawns, a swimming pool. Kids' paradise. But you approach it with some wariness. Are you afraid?"

Yes.

"Can you tell me what of?" The analyst leaned over her, and Ivy Day welcomed the dissection.

She rose. She shook out her hair. She surveyed this room, grand, filled with Georgia O'Keefe originals and first edition books and silk and leather upholstery. Only a few were permitted entrance into her sanctuaries—and the magazines drooled over it. She opened her mouth and said that she was afraid of one day having to go back to that.

"Back to that?" the analyst repeated. "To childhood?"

No.

"Back to the yard?"

Yes.

"The pool?"

Yes.

"The small house?"

Yes.

"Being called Mary?"

Yes. Back to all that. It would kill Ivy Day if she had to go back to all that.

JOHN MARK shaved his head. It had all begun to fall out in his late teens, and the hair left was a dull wax color, not blond as it had been before.

He stood in the shower, before he turned on the water, and ran the length of the electric razor's cord from its plug by the sink. He loved this ritual, this part of the morning before he had fully awoken. There wasn't much on his head to get rid of, but the mowing of the blades clipped away, with the hair, any flakes of skin that he would otherwise have to scrub off.

Scalp done, he moved to the rest of himself, jaw, chest, arms, legs, the wiry thicket at his groin. He'd begun to shear himself not long after his first meeting at Hooray for Hollywood Video. He wanted to be smooth, top to bottom.

The day after he'd begun this part of the ritual, someone at work noticed his bare forearm. Someone else saw a hairless calf when he bent to tie his shoe. People asked, "You training for the Olympics? You going to be the new Bruce Jenner?" This was a real joke because JOHN MARK had all the prowess of a pussy willow.

He looked at his feet. The base of the shower-and-bathtub was littered with fur. If anyone who made jokes at him knew what it was to shed some part of themselves, they might not find it so funny. People lost weight, people dyed their hair, people had their faces resculpted.

It was what they did at the morgue sometimes. People couldn't bear to have their dead returned to them as what they were now, as meat. It was not the custom of a morgue to do this. The reconstruction and makeup processes were normally left to the funeral home. But some of the dieners were happy to do it, once the bodies had been claimed. It was the part of his job that JOHN MARK loved.

Today, he'd worked on a woman who had been found in her neighbor's garage. Late into the night before, she'd slipped in and hotwired the Ford sedan. She'd been huddled in the backseat of the car, the engine filling the space with fumes. For maybe half a day, her air had been nothing but spirituous murk. JOHN MARK had thought she looked drunk when they brought her in, from the way her face sagged. The collectors hadn't closed her eyes, and until JOHN MARK could do it himself, she'd gazed at him from the steel washing table with something that seemed close to awe. She had her dark hair knotted at the top of her head, and the tightness of it pulled at the skin of her forehead, her brows. Maybe she was a girl—she looked young enough.

She wasn't pretty.

She hadn't even tried.

He lathered up, gloved his hands. He was alone with her and, since the cause of her demise had been worked out, her mother ushered in to nod and weep and ushered out again, he could doll her up.

He shampooed her hair. He kept his own supply in his locker, Ivy Day's 2-in-1 coconut and shea butter. He could spare a bit for her; already she carried a stink. JOHN MARK hummed and filled the air with bubbles and good aromas.

Sometimes, when the mood was right, when the dead weren't feeling too self-conscious, he could talk to them. It wasn't hard, he was surprised that more dieners didn't try it. JOHN MARK introduced himself. Then, he bent over the suds and asked, "What's your name? I didn't catch yours when they brought you in."

You had to have a good ear to hear the dead. Usually, all you could make out were rusty sounds, delicate cords beginning to slow, then freeze. He'd had to ask again.

Then, in the manner of a ventriloquist, from between her teeth, her lips moving only a bit: "Mary."

JOHN MARK blinked. He'd known a Mary once, somewhere. He knew a lot of Marys. He didn't want to think that this one might be different from the others. His hand shook when he bent to drain the table. "How old are you?"

"Fifteen," the girl muttered. Her voice was claggy.

He wound a length of tubing down her throat to drain bile and other refuse. Then, he emptied it into a bucket.

Her voice was clearer when she whispered, "Thank you."

"You're welcome." JOHN MARK plugged in the hairdryer. "Let me know if it's too hot."

"I donno." The girl sounded as though she were in a stupor. "I donno." He heard her over the roar of the hairdryer.

"What made you do it?" JOHN MARK didn't worry about intrusiveness on his part. What was Mary going to do?

When dried, her hair puffed, cloudlike, around her head and shoulders. Before, what had escaped from her knot had been stringy and slick before the morgue had gotten to her. She was nearly pretty. Still, she said, "I donno."

JOHN MARK moved to her nails. He began to clean them, for the undersides were packed with grime, the rose pink polish chipped. At the end, she hadn't been taking care of herself. His clippers were sharp, precise. His eye was keen. "No," he said, "come on. What made you do it?"

JOHN MARK hovered over her, so that she could see him (or so he could believe that she could see him). Her eyes were between grey and green. "Come on," he coaxed. What might he have said to her, if he were anyone else? *You had so much to live for? Nothing is ever as bad as it seems?* It was a bit late for all that, now, and he wasn't a natural soother, to the living or the dead. He fed off this stuff. He simply wanted to know.

Now and then, when a hint of pressure was put on the body (even a gust from the air vent could do it), the one on the table would let out a sound that was close to a groan. New dieners were scared out of their minds when they heard it. Louder than you would expect, at first a monotone, before petering out in a ragged gnarr that undulated, then cracked, then silenced. It was probably where the vampire myth came from, all those villagers digging up graves, hitting the departed in the chest with the brunt of their shovels. There were still vocal cords, and there was still air trapped inside.

Nevertheless, JOHN MARK leapt away when that horrible noise rose from Mary's chest.

"God," he panted. "Don't do that."

It rose again, softer this time, almost a squeak. The air vent had kicked in to keep the room cool. Mary seemed chilled, at any rate. When JOHN MARK lifted her head to brush the hair, he noted the pooling of color on the underside, like one, big bruise. It made the rest of her seem yellow. She was stiffening, and in time, she would freeze completely. What good was a colossus, if she could not speak?

He asked again, "What made you do it?"

He hadn't yet closed her eyes. She did not flinch, even though, this late in his career, he half expected the bodies to do so when he made them up. This was a "memory picture", as they called it, restoring the face of the deceased to the way it had been in life. He would leave the cosmetics to the funeral home. He dipped into a container of Ivy Day's new product, a massage crème that smelled of vanilla. This would rehydrate the tissue, enough to make her appear comatose, if not asleep.

"What made you do it?" JOHN MARK was not rubbing the stuff in, but slapping. Again and again and again. Even as he did it, he wondered at why he cared, what was it to him. But it was her own fault, as it was everyone's own fault who came through here. He stopped when he saw the marks he was making on her cheeks. Now that her blood did not circulate, they would not fade. He rushed to cover it, massage the cheeks, layer the crème on thick. The room was wide and cold, yet the vanilla odor prevailed. It was like being gassed by pastry.

At last, when he thought she might have frozen for good, he heard her moan, so soft and crackling, "It was a boy."

"A boy?"

"Boy. That's all."

"What? He didn't love you?"

"That's right." She sounded as though she were being pulled tighter and tighter. Sooner or later, she would break and go. "Stupid now."

"Do you wish you hadn't done it?"

Then came her last word. "Yeah."

And she went still and that was all. THE END.

JOHN MARK, in another time or in another place, might have agreed. Yes, that was a stupid thing to do, a silly girl throwing herself into some hole for a boy whose name she might forget in another ten years.

But what if you don't forget?

There are people (Ivy Day Ivy Day Ivy Day) whom you cannot forget. You see them, and their face, their voice, cuts into your brain and leaves a scar.

Ivy Day.

Ivy Day.

Ivy Day.

He thought the name in threes as he made up dead Mary's face. He'd spare some of his best crème for her.

Ivy Day.

Ivy Day.

Ivy Day.

There was a movie on TV tonight.

There was a marathon on TV tonight. The girls wouldn't miss it for anything. From eight o'clock until midnight, AMC was hosting five of Ivy Day's films, from her breakthrough feature (*Piñata*) to *SS Clelia*. They congregated again at Celeste's because she had gotten her own television for her sixteenth birthday and her parents would be out for the evening. They would have the place to themselves.

The girls arrived at seven and abandoned their coats and shoes by the door. That done, the three stood a minute in the foyer, sponging the new quiet of the house. It was not their first occasion having the house to themselves, and it was not their first sleepover. But they were new friends; they had been thrown together only last year as freshmen and now, as per the notion of predestination, it seemed that they were meant to be together. They ate together. They orchestrated nightly three-way phone calls. There were testaments to their friendship, tokens in photo booth snapshots, matching bracelets. They had never slept in the same room, had never seen each other unclothed. Though they had seen one another weep (Celeste and Brooke would never forget Adrienne's shrieks over the bleach), it felt unlikely that they excreted, or even smelled bad. It was a big step, letting each other in like this.

And now they would worship together.

They all knew that they were fans of Ivy Day. Lots of people were, and there was no shame in that. It was all a matter of revealing just how devoted you were that could bring you from normality to gross aberration. *I love Ivy Day.* Say it with too much reverence and people had a picture of you alone, pasting magazine cuttings to your bathroom wall, when you weren't writing fan ardent letters. In the girls' defense, they hadn't gotten quite that bad; at least, they weren't writing letters.

And yet it was delicious, harboring this common love. This secret, their shining knowledge.

They moved around each other, coy, fixing snacks, going in and out of the fridge, in and out of the pantry. They were going to have a feast, because the next day they were going on a diet. And so, they would indulge as much as they could now, the way you would in the days preceding Lent. Brooke had brought a pan of homemade fudge and two bags of kettle corn. Adrienne, whose mother was a hobby baker, had staggered in under the weight of a Tupperware box holding two dozen chocolate peanut butter bars. ("They're not all for you," Adrienne's mother had said. "Save some for the family, please.") They were going to fix savories. In the kitchen, they found dill pickles, bags of corn chips, two kinds of salsa (tomato and pineapple), slices of ham, cheddar cheese for their peanut butter bars ("It sounds disgusting, but together they taste so good," Adrienne insisted.). In the refrigerator, there were cans of root beer and (because they had the house to themselves) a slim bottle of ice wine Celeste's parents had picked up in Niagara Falls. They toasted with juice glasses, and giggled at their puckering lips. Brooke sniffed and said, "It's like that sugar water you leave out for humming birds."

And it loosened them.

They had some time to spare before the marathon began. Commercials ran and they sat on the floor of Celeste's bedroom, nibbling and not quite looking at one another. They wondered how the faithful found other faithfuls. Before the Fall of Rome, early Christians used the sign of the fish. Freemasons had secret handshakes. How do you show yourself?

Celeste's eyes itched. She couldn't be the only one. She resisted rubbing, or else the mascara would smear. It was comforting to know that she was not the only one. Ennobling, in fact, to see that Brooke and Adrienne blinked, squinted, red-rimmed and a little teary. And no one stopped to scratch. Every now and then, one of the girls would stop and look another of them in the eye, catching a hand that might rise, a probing finger. They'd worked so hard for their look.

In Celeste's room, they gathered before the television. It was a tiny thing, made in Osaka and just light enough to fit on the middle shelf of Celeste's bookcase. It intermittently fuzzed in and out from color to black and white, but the girls could move past this, for the picture was otherwise clear. *My Lilac* had started; in it, Ivy Day played two identical women who, unbeknownst to one another, are next door neighbors. They have the same name, the same birthday, et cetera. Also, unbeknownst to the two Lilacs, they have friends in common. Eventually, everyone the Lilacs know catch on and take advantage of the two women in different ways: A dear friend steals, a lover philanders, and so on. And what the two Lilacs come to know when they finally meet is that they are the other's soulmate, the one in the world whom they can give their trust and their hearts to.

The Double Life of Veronique. Partner. Persona. People liked to point out which movies about doubles had been lifted from and watered down to make *My Lilac.*

People liked to show off.

People weren't as highbrowed as they thought they were.

People were stupid.

People surrendered to the comfort of easy cinema and beautiful starlets who died and came back, film after film, just for them. They would rather die than admit it.

The Double Life of Veronique was in Polish and French. *Partner* was in Italian. *Persona* was in Swedish. Was it because *My Lilac* was in English?

Of course, the girls cried when the movie ended. The two Lilacs are discovered to be the ex-lovers of their mutual ex-boyfriend. The mutual ex-boyfriend owed money to a passel of wiseguys, and thought he might divert them by telling them that they could collect their due from the Lilacs. The Lilacs, moments after having found each other on a public basketball court, each having recognized her other, are shot—one bullet through both heads.

It was a beautiful death. And it was a beautiful thing to cry, not just for itself, for you could not pull yourself from the picture and its environs until long after the credits had ended. It wasn't so much the picture you cried for; Ivy Day was the kind of actress you thought of for days afterward. Sometimes she played the hero. Other times, she played someone like you, a pretty, poised, precious variant that did not seem so unattainable, now that you had seen it for yourself.

In time, the girls found peace and were still.

JOHN MARK was at the supermarket. It was the HEB a few blocks from where he lived. He'd thought it would be a quick trip, cereal, milk, peppers, rice. It might have been any other day, so routine as to never have happened.

It was something he'd think on quite a bit, later. Principally, what he would think about was that if he had been more careful, if he'd not been so scattered, this day might not have happened, and what was to grow within him and to come, as a result, would not have happened.

He had no one to blame but himself, at the end of it.

JOHN MARK was at the supermarket. It was the HEB a few blocks from where he lived. He steered a cart and collected cereal, milk, peppers, rice. At one point in between getting the cereal and the rice, he stopped by the florist's corner. There had been a bunch of blue hydrangeas that had caught his eye the last time had been here, and since that last trip he'd read in *Elle Décor* that Ivy Day's ornaments of choice were flowers, specifically hydrangeas, specifically blue ones. There were hydrangeas at the florists, but they were fake, as it turned out. It had only taken him until he'd reached the cash register with them that he found they had no odor and had little softness.

Perhaps that was where he had lost his debit card.

He'd gotten the cereal, the milk, the peppers, the rice. He had gotten a place in the shortest line, and he had very nearly checked out, receipt ready and flapping from a gangly boy's hand, when he saw that his wallet was empty and his debit card was missing.

"I can take cash," the gangly boy said, helpless.

JOHN MARK hadn't any cash. JOHN MARK had thought he wouldn't need any cash because he would have his debit card. He told this to the gangly boy, whose face quickly maneuvered from helpless to flustered. JOHN MARK remembered that he must be generous, as Ivy Day was. He took a breath and, after counting to ten, recounted what had happened: the florist's, the fake hydrangeas, the milk, peppers and rice, the debit card gone.

The gangly boy brightened. "I can call over to the florist's. That's probably where you lost it."

JOHN MARK began to burn, somewhere in his bowels. It was probably not true, but the thought persisted: The gangly boy blamed JOHN MARK. *That's probably where you lost it.* And the boy had not brightened, not out of any helpfulness; he wanted only for JOHN MARK to go away.

The woman from the florists appeared and she smelled. She had a card, clipped between her fingers, and she tried to give it to JOHN MARK with a flourish, but her hands were slick with lotion and it dropped to the floor. "I found it behind the poinsettias," she smirked. JOHN MARK flapped her away; it took him four or five grabs before he had it, before he could squint and see that while the card was a Visa, like his, and the names matched his, the spelling was off. JON MARK. He moved to hand it back to the woman, and the card slipped once, twice, thrice, four times...

When she caught it, she had to snatch it from him. When she righted herself, she tapped the gangly fellow on the shoulder. It seemed that she had some capacity in the daily close-outs and lost and found items. "We get all kinds of stuff at the end of a day. One time, Andre found a glass eye in with the bath beads. With credit cards, when we get that kind of stuff, we lock it up in the safe 'til someone claims it." The gangly boy sauntered away, twirling the keys on one finger. (JOHN MARK wondered if he was Andre, and if he was, had he kept the glass eye for himself?)

The woman from the florist was good, was kind. Perhaps she saw some golden quality in JOHN MARK. Perhaps, more likely, though he was quick to suffocate it, she was sorry for him. He'd caught his reflection through her bifocals: small, and he trembled, a fellow with a short fuse. He saw, too, when he looked down, that his nails had chipped. He did not know when he had been led away from the main part of the store, for it seemed that the walls had folded in, the lights had dimmed, and here he was, situated in a red plastic chair. Off to the side, in the corridor between the restroom and the employees' entrance to the credit union. He had a paper cup of water in one hand, half-emptied.

At his feet were four debit cards, all Visas.

JOHN MARKE

JON D. MARK

JEAN MARC

JOHN MERKE

The numbers were off by a digit. The cards expired in the same year as his, in a different month, or the same month, in a different year. One of the cards had been dead for a month.

"Where are my things?" he asked. He let the cup of water go and it spilled across his lap. "Where are my things? My rice..."

No one was talking to him. They were talking at him. They were telling him to calm down. They were telling him to take a breath, take a drink. JOHN MARK obeyed. Someone, the gangly Andre, was hovering in the hallway's darker segment, in the company of a man in blue. Gangly Andre seemed on edge that there was only one man in blue, and he hid behind the uniformed man's bulk.

JOHN MARK turned to look out into the store. He saw bags strewn and torn, but otherwise everything appeared orderly. It was when the man in blue escorted him (nearly held JOHN

MARK's hand, he did) to his car that he beheld the true extent of his temper:

The florist's, in shreds.

The banana pyramid, dismantled.

The floor, streaked, skidmarked, scuffed.

The shoppers, aghast.

One of them called out, "Motherfucker thrown fruit at me."

JOHN MARK did not hear the rest. He had a vague memory of having seen these things, the flowers, the bananas, the bags. Perhaps his shoes had made those marks, though he couldn't have said how. The flowers, the bananas, the bags were props in another, less important life. He was not wont to say that it was truly his. For despite his apparent frenzy, he was abandoned at his car by the man in blue with nothing more than a good talking-to. No arrest. No probing at his well-being. None of that. The flowers, the bananas, the bags would return to their places, and what got damaged would be thrown out. People would talk about that fellow who lost his mind at HEB, as though it were a headline, and then they wouldn't. Time would pass. JOHN MARK could eventually return to that HEB, anytime he wanted, perhaps as soon as tomorrow. And if he did have another conniption, he thought, driving home, if he put on another show, bigger and gaudier and louder, the same would happen again. The flowers, the bananas, the bags, the man in blue, gangly Andre or Wesley or Tyler, whoever was on shift, maybe the eyeball in the bath beads. And maybe the new debit card would be the start of it. And the one after.

JOHN MARK would be erased.

He got home.

From the television, Ivy Day greeted him, her movie from five years ago, *All My Pretty Ones*, an adaptation of Anne Sexton's life and poems, not quite a biopic. Anne Sexton committed suicide on October 4th, 1974. She turned on her car in her sealed garage, wrapped in a fur coat and a glut of vodka. Ivy Day was Anne Sexton to her dying breath. The screen went black, but for small letters: *Whether you are pretty or not, I outlive you/Bend down my strange face to yours and forgive you.*

Because this was an Ivy Day marathon, she came back from the dead for her next film, *American Fruit.*

You couldn't make it in movies without doing one picture that had the word AMERICAN in the title. *American Psycho. American Beauty. American Heart. American Pie.*

American Fruit was the good one.

An earworm, he let the shopper's voice replay itself. *Motherfucker thrown fruit at me.* It was without relief that tomorrow or the next day people would have forgotten all about it. He listened awhile more, then got up to the ding of the microwave. His tea was ready. He had it with a plate of sliced apples and a dollop of peanut butter; Ivy Day had said somewhere that this was her favorite snack.

Time passed and it was midnight. One of Ivy Day's campier movies was on, a psychedelic musical, *Discophrenia*, co-starring Uma Thurman and Whitney Houston. Whitney Houston was dead; they would never let you forget it, for if they didn't, you would never remember that she had lived. At the morgue, every other song on the radio was "One Moment in Time". People grieved for days, left flowers at the Beverly Hilton Hotel, as though they had known her, and she them. Uma Thurman was something else, living, though you would never guess. It had been awhile since JOHN MARK had seen her anywhere, onscreen or in magazines. In time, he thought, he might forget her, and knowing this was truly satisfying.

Knowing this was truly satisfying.

On the television, he saw Ivy Day and he saw Whitney Huston, but he did not see Uma Thurman. The movie had reached its climax and she might well have disappeared. This was how gods died and how the current Almighty would die: Seasons as eons, accolades, tales, epics, fixing themselves within human cognizance as stars. It was very on-the-nose, JOHN MARK knew (so suddenly, his breath came short), to call these people, these golden people, stars. Because (at this, his breath came shorter) stars burn out, don't they, long before they disappear. Seasons as eons. Take Orson Welles, director, writer, lead of a picture that everyone in cinema, whether they like it or not, finds themselves compared to. JOHN MARK read it all the time in the magazines: *The Citizen Kane of bad movies. The Citizen Kane of its generation. The Citizen Kane of kung-fu.* And damn it if at the end of his life Orson Welles was doing commercials for frozen peas. He had grown fat. He was a drunk. He had lapped up devotion too fast. He died, of all things, from a heart attack.

Only peons died from heart attacks.

JOHN MARK felt his circulation, a thrumming that began at his breast and seemed to suck the blood from his brain with every pulse. He put his head between his knees. Meanwhile, the TV had gone fuzzy. This was the hour when all shows stopped and left a fuzzy screen until six AM. He murmured apologies to Orson Welles. Though his star was a ghost, JOHN MARK reasoned that it still counted as blasphemy.

It was sad enough for ordinary people to have to be born and buried so quickly. What about the golden ones? That must be like watching your own decomposition, mustn't it? And sometimes your fans weren't always so faithful. There were dissenters in every crowd, the ones who took pleasure in another's fall. Of Orson Welles, JOHN MARK had a distinct memory of himself, looking at a picture of the great man in his youth, and another taken during Welles' frozen peas era. "God," JOHN MARK remembered saying, "he got fat." Never mind the Oscars. Here was the *Citizen Kane* of lard.

He painted his toenails and he resolved to cut milk from his diet.

They painted their toenails and they resolved to cut milk from their diet. For it was in an interview with *Good Earth Lifestyles* that Ivy Day had claimed the key to clear skin was nixing the dairy.

The girls had been slicing her interviews from magazines, on beauty, on style, on health, on morality. And they had folders with labels, interviews archived by date and topic. They had gotten so that they could quote from them as one might from sacred text. Ivy Day had said in *Nylon*, "My fans can live without me. I can't live without my fans." Adrienne debated having that tattooed around her wrist, to the awe of Brooke and Celeste. But Ivy Day hadn't any tattoos, and so the plan was dropped.

They were at the bathroom in the park. The park itself backed up to a shopping center, and it serviced the outpour of patrons with children. Before going on to the duck pond and the large-as-life granite cow sculptures, mothers wove through with little girls. Little girls were the ones who watched, as

Adrienne and Brooke and Celeste had watched Ivy Day. *Except ye be converted, and become as little children.* Becoming a big girl seemed then a day that may never come. It was visible, for you could see other girls, real ones who had been let to transubstantiate. There was no knowing if it might happen to you.

Adrienne and Brooke and Celeste knew this, and they took the time to smile at the little girl in the big buckled sandals. She had been following their hands, which knew how to sculpt hair, paint eyes and lips wide and blooming. Their pores were small. Their clothes were without smudge or crease. If they could see themselves as the little girl saw them.

If they could see themselves at all.

It was Brooke who had first said it aloud: "It itches."

Adrienne and Celeste had asked, "What does?", as though they did not know. To say it would make it real. They had already trained their hands away from their faces, Adrienne by sitting on them, Celeste by jabbing herself, once, in the eye with her manicure. She hadn't seen out of that eye for a week, and the agony was a welcome meditation.

Brooke remained the realist. "The liner. The shadow. It's making me tear up. I can't see."

Adrienne's hand twitched and she made a ball of it. Celeste readied hers into a claw, willing to take out both eyes if need be. No denying, it was terrible, even under cold cream, or washed away with soap and water. It was a burden that did not let them sleep for the scratching. But scratching tore away their lashes. What could you do?

Brooke had wept, which made it worse. And her liner was turning to grime. "I can't see. I can't seeeee—" She rubbed her cheeks, streaking them black. She wailed. "I can't seeeeee!"

Adrienne sighed. Beside her, Celeste's face went tight. To Adrienne, the world held brightness and colors and shapes. She was the one who read from the magazines and who translated from images into words the movies that played on TV. Celeste beheld light and dark, a certain foam of red or yellow. She traveled by smell, and knew the number of steps from her house to Adrienne's, her house to Brooke's.

And Brooke. For Brooke, there were no colors. She had scratched until the kohl had worked into her sight with dirt. For a week, her eyes leaked a milky ooze, to be sponged away with tissues every quarter-hour. People at school asked, "What's she crying for?" Adrienne never told anyone, certainly not poor Brooke, of the crust that would form if she did not blot and apply coat after coat of Ivy Day's liquid foundation beneath the bottom lids. Then followed the mascara, that which came for her eyes in the first place. Brooke had always been the most competent when it came to liner and shadow, she could do a cat-eye with her eyes closed. Now she could do it blind.

She could paint all of them, dependent on her fingers to keep a golden symmetry, her mind's eye (though deteriorating to smeary memory) to know which shades would match which skin. She applied iridescence and luster, inky streaks and layers of lashes like feathers. The ooze added shine and, when it dried, shimmer. In time, you could not see the eye for itself.

In school, they walked three abreast, like something out of a movie. Adrienne took the center, flanked by Celeste and Brooke, who knew to look ahead, aloof, mouths pursed and bitten red when the lipstick ran out. They were discreet about where they gripped Adrienne's jacket; they did not want to look like followers.

In fact, it was Adrienne who would follow, in a way.

Brooke said, out of the blue, "She's wearing burgundy thigh-highs."

Adrienne had been reading to them from the day's issue of *Glamour*. She paused. Ivy Day was the cover feature. In New York, she had worn a pair of wine-colored boots to a Kenzo show during Fashion Week. They zipped up the back, hugging the leg all the way around almost like a stocking, and the heels were stacked in platform wedges. No one had worn thigh-high boots since the seventies, and suddenly everyone had to have them. The attributions were made to Ivy Day, as opposed to the designer.

And that was the killer of it. No one knew who had made the boots. The photographs in the magazines were taken mid-action, Ivy Day walking into the show, Ivy Day walking out of the show, Ivy Day on the arm of Peter Gabriel, who wore a flowing topcoat that, to many a fan's chagrin, swept across Ivy Day's legs, obscuring the boots. It was anyone's guess, really, but a few armchair detectives had narrowed the material down to satin or leather, based on the glare in the photographs.

"They're both wrong," Brooke intoned. "It's velvet."

Celeste sniffed. She treasured the little sight she had and made use of it scouring the magazines for details. She kept a magnifying glass in her handbag and talked about getting a monocle. Impatient, she held the *Glamour* issue close to her face; her lashes whipped against the page. "How do you figure that?" She handed the magazine to Adrienne. "The pictures weren't even that good."

Adrienne looked. When she did, she eyed Brooke, who said as though it were written, in the Bible as well as *Glamour*, "Ivy Day is vegan."

Celeste puzzled, then gasped. "Okay, right. They don't wear leather." She wondered how Brooke had come to know this. Last the world heard, Ivy Day had only nixed dairy from her diet.

Adrienne nodded. "And satin is a silk product. And vegans don't contribute to the exploitation of silkworms." She imagined a sweatshop, silkworms standing elbow to elbow. Or tail to tail. It saddened her.

It saddened all of them. They had been eating Honey Nut Cheerios. The mistreatment of honeybees must be through the roof. They took their hands from the box and were not tempted to lick their fingers.

"Couldn't it be fake leather, or something?" Celeste sat on her hands.

Brooke's eyes never blinked. She was the one who sat in the patch of sun that fell through Celeste's bedroom window, bathed in light that she knew of but could not see, like an oracle. "She wouldn't wear something that cheap." She did not need to say more.

Brooke knew more than that. She knew that Ivy Day had let her hair return to its natural wave, after more than a year of ironing and angled trimming. The maker of the boots remained undisclosed, as they were custom-fit and a private gift. She was in New York at the time of the article, of course, but by the time it went to print she was at her home in California, in a hamlet called Angels Camp. "It's like where I grew up," she'd said when asked why she would think to live in such a little town. "Most actors like to set up house closer to work," the interviewer had noted. Ivy Day answered by saying that home was where the heart is. *Glamour* then asked where home was, "Originally. We know it's reminiscent of Angels Camp." Ivy Day told the magazine that there were a lot of places in the world like Angels Camp, and went on to discuss her new film, *Mother Lode Acres*, now in post-production.

All this appeared one month later, in an issue of *Women's Health* announcing Ivy Day's "life-changing" move to veganism. Tofu, seitan, jackfruit, edamame, protein powder, portabella, tempeh, almond milk, nutritional yeast, cacao, wheatgrass, brown rice, avocado, and cauliflower in all its applications. Things that the girls had never touched they hungered for, or pretended to. Adrienne discovered that many of their favorite foods were vegan, and so they lived off Oreos, Bac-O's bacon bits, Duncan Hines cake frosting, marshmallows, Pop-Tarts, Ritz crackers, Airheads, Fruit by the Foot, Fritos corn chips, tortilla chips, Hershey's syrup, and Clif Bars in every flavor.

As a result, the girls looked great and felt horrible. They were sick at the beginning and the end of each day, with a sudden, jolting crash in the afternoon. They experienced palpitations. Their mouths were dry; to remedy this, they sucked on buttons pulled off coats, for they didn't know if breath mints were vegan, and water seemed to evaporate as fast as it could meet their tongues. There were upsides to it, however. The richness of their diet, the hedonistic excesses of sugar and salt, made them eat in tablespoons. They lost more weight than they ever had eating vegetables. The sickness that came in the mornings and evenings caused them to purge it all from their bodies, and the crash brought them to a hazy plateau.

This became their favorite part of the day; colors brightened, sounds echoed. Brooke said that she could hear a window opening on the other side of town. Adrienne, blessed with sight, told them of the yellows in the clouds, the reds in the shadows at day's end. These were things that Celeste could see, and she claimed that the colors had a sound, the yellow like the snapping of fingers, the red like guitar strings. They had discovered an entire universe, fragile and intricate, superimposed upon the one they knew. Brooke, who had grown up Catholic, talked about the Thin Place, where the boundaries between men and angels blurred, where the anointed heard the call of the saints, and where martyrs received stigmata. You never knew where to find the Thin Place, but it was one of those things that you would know when you saw it.

Celeste sniffed, "So then Adrienne can tell us."

Brooke reminded her of that Ivy Day movie, one of her early ones, called *Lux*. They had seen it last weekend (or, Adrienne had followed the action and described it for Celeste and Brooke). Ivy Day was a blind woman, a concert flutist with synesthesia. Notes appeared and colors sounded, Technicolor blooms that flared just behind Ivy Day's head when she played. And she had played; she studied the flute in under a year and had become so good that the New York Philharmonic offered her a place. And she had gone blind; during the first week of shooting, she'd worn contact lenses so thick that her corneas were scratched. She refused surgery until the film had gone into post-production.

(Parenthetically, during that time, sunglasses with very big lenses were In. Having once been called Jackie O's, the name changed to I.D.s, as though Jackie Onassis had been the one to steal the look from Ivy Day.)

Now that Brooke and Celeste were blind, they relied on what they could recall from before, and what they could conjure for themselves. Celeste said that, now that they were no longer bothered by the ugliness in the world, they could see anything they liked. "Poor Angie," she laughed, and Adrienne threatened to leave the two of them wandering around and around the supermarket.

Did Ivy Day see them, in her mind's eye, as they saw her?

"She has to," Brooke said. They were in the frozen foods aisle, debating whether or not to break their vegan fast and get some Halo Top ice cream. The vanilla bean flavor was only two hundred-and-eighty calories per pint. "Per pint," she echoed when Adrienne read that to her. Then, she straightened. "No. Come on. Let's find the Rice Dream."

She and Celeste fell into line. Celeste patted her thigh, once, twice, a third time roughly. "Hut-hut, Angie." She clicked her teeth. "An-*gie*. Let's go."

And for a minute, Adrienne was quiet. They were calling her by her ugly name, the one given in honor of a fusty great aunt, not one that Adrienne, nor anyone, would have chosen for herself. It was the name of some greasy-haired know-nothing who would become nothing, who pretended that glamour didn't matter because it was the thing she wanted most—and would never get. It was a dog's name. And the long version wasn't any better: On paper, she was Angela. Not Angelina, not Anjelica. Her mother had liked *Murder, She Wrote*, and that was where she'd found it. Old people watched *Murder, She Wrote*. Old people loved Angela Lansbury. If Angie stunk of dog, Angela reeked of mothballs. You might as well have named your little girl Ethel or Gertrude.

"An-*gie*." Celeste's voice was a drill. She wore a tight little smirk and, though she couldn't see and Brooke couldn't either, they turned their faces to each other, smiling. "An-geeee—" Since before, they had always had that one on her. Crystal and

Becky were a dime a dozen, and that was always better than a grandmother's name.

Adrienne swallowed. She knew, she always knew. They could say the ugliest things, or neglect her entirely. They could pull her fingernails, one by one, and she would turn the other cheek. She always had before.

But they had called her Angie.

On top of all that.

Well. See how you'll like it.

She was glad that she had worn her soft-soled shoes. The Adidas ones, strips of navy down the sides, taking one step back, and then another. Celeste and Brooke grew smaller. When they grew smaller, they grew sillier; they held themselves very stiffly, now that they had no guide dog. Celeste pawed the air, found Brooke's sleeve. Her free hand groped until she thought she'd got hold of Adrienne. The look on her face when the old woman whose sweatshirt she'd tugged brushed her away, barking, "Get off. Sober up."

They were going to cry. They were not going to cry this instant, or even the next minute, but they were going to cry. Celeste, going red. Brooke, going white. There was sweat and chills, so much so that the girls' perfume grew tainted with stink, and Adrienne could feel the vibrations from where she stood by the granola aisle. It shook her, the way it might if she were receiving electrical shocks every other minute. Being a dog had made her too loyal. Meanwhile, Celeste and Brooke had given up pawing and began to call, first steadily, then in panic when Adrienne did not come.

It was awful; people were staring. And for a minute, the sympathy ebbed and Adrienne could see what they saw: two stalks of girls, beautiful, primped, unable to find their way out of a grocery store. Here was compensation; the girls were gorgeous but with one marshmallow-brain between the two of them. This was cosmic justice, proof of some kind of order. In a world where the prettiest get everything, they ought to be denied something, just one thing. A few people laughed.

Adrienne knew she shouldn't. She laughed, too.

At last, Celeste and Brooke, shriveled into the creatures known as Crystal and Becky. Crystal and Becky could break. The change was so sudden that they could hardly breathe. Their desires were without abstract. They wanted to go home. They wanted to be warm. They wanted their mothers.

Adrienne decided that when they cried, she would come.

JOHN MARK put a television in at the morgue, so he could watch while he worked. It was a small make, found at a RadioShack clearance. *My Lilac* was on. You could almost count on it being on, like *The Shawshank Redemption*. He was hosing down the table. Lately, much of what he did was hose down the table, wash the instruments. He no longer dealt with the bodies, as he had been careless.

He'd worked on another girl. Her name was Mary. He knew that her name was Mary because she'd told him so, this time as he filled her emptied skull with plaster. She'd been careless, too, having disengaged her attentions from the road to her car radio.

"That song was on again," she said. It came out dry, less than a moan.

"What song?" The plaster was pumped in through a hose, powered by a foot pedal on the floor. It was hard to hear, but JOHN MARK kept his head low. Now and then, his lips would dip to touch her earlobe.

"That song."

"There's a lot of songs."

She croaked, no words. In a while, the stuff inside, that pneumatic fog, would evaporate and she would be gone. JOHN MARK suggested that she sing a bit of it.

"Can't sing."

"Say it, then."

Nothing compares 2 U...

It was on all the time. Sinead O'Connor would never be known for anything else, but at least she could be an earworm. And it wasn't even her song. Lyrics penned in diaries, on school notebooks, tattooed on kids' rubbery arms. Flip the stations and you'd find it. Maybe it serenaded a shampoo commercial.

Nothing compares 2 U...

Mary sighed. "Don't remember the rest. It's on all the time. Don't remember."

"You wanted a different song."

"Wanted a different song."

There was plaster in her hair. He sponged it away.

"Anything else you wanted?"

Mary moaned. "Wanted love."

There was plaster in her ear, foaming down the grey canal. He wedged it out.

"Whose love?"

Mary went quiet. Then, in one burst, the volume just above a whisper: "Don't remember."

And that was all. It would be wrong to call it sudden, for there is always something left of everyone, a word, a smell, a color—most often a thought, elliptical, obsessive. The thoughts were what could catch you the most, for they ought to be simple and they hung around longer than smells.

This might have been when JOHN MARK heard it on the television. Maybe he read it in a magazine, or caught a bit of conversation in line at the HEB. He didn't know who had said it or where. But he knew, the way Adam knew God when he saw Him, the way you know that the sky is blue.

Ivy Day was coming to town.

Ivy Day was making a new film.

Ivy Day was coming to town to make a new film.

Ivy Day was coming to town to make the film of her career.

Ivy Day was coming to town to make the film of her career, and she was looking for locals.

Ivy Day was coming to town to make the film of her career, and she was looking for locals to cast as extras.

Since you been gone, I can do whatever I want...

Meanwhile, JOHN MARK's foot on the pedal was heavy. Plaster leaked from Mary's ears.

vy Day had trained from dawn until half-eight. She consumed a concoction of almond butter, plums, kale, coconut oil and bok choy and swam thirty lengths. She then went on to her appointment with the same yogi who had previously worked with Sting. When she began, she could hardly do a split (she said for *Women's Fit*). Now she could support herself on her elbows while touching her toes to her shoulders (she said for *Vogue*). She ate a bowl of kelp noodles seasoned with tamari and sesame seeds, garnished with shredded carrot and chickpeas. She did not believe in counting calories, for counting calories led to eating disorders. However, she did not allow herself sugar, not anymore.

These were her meals. This was her routine. Her meals and routine, as many knew, were apt to change, according to a new role.

There was a lot of buzz about this one. Cardio and stretching, vegetables, high fiber. She was slimming down from *Portals*, for which she had gained twenty pounds of muscle. (Her right hand, owing to "thematic and artistic necessity" [she said for *Fantasmagoria*], had been rendered useless. There are twenty-seven bones in the human hand. When shattered, the appendage reminds its master that this is what is to become of her, that she is only meat. While *Portals* was in post-production, Ivy Day was fitted for a prosthetic, the best of its kind, unavailable to the public. It was programmed to mark her signature, down to the loops of the Ys. But this was a rumor. Someone thought the space between her thumb and forefinger had seemed off, and the idea in some circles took root.) People had speculations. It was too soon since *Black Swan* for another ballet picture. Maybe a sinewy role, like a mermaid? Ivy Day had always taken to fantasy. If it were a fantasy film, she could be anything. A mermaid, an angel, an elf, a faerie queen.

What would bring a faerie queen to a town like this? You went to New Zealand to make a film like that, not here.

Would the locals be cast as hobbits?

Regardless, the Summit was pre-selling tickets to the new Ivy Day flick.

t's not a fantasy." Brooke had spoken, so it must be true. Adrienne and Celeste sighed. "Thank God." Celeste reached to make sure Adrienne was still at her side. She was. "We won't have to wear those ugly-ass feet."

Adrienne asked, "What? What are you even talking about?" It was easier to talk back now. And she was beginning to know how good it felt. *Now it's me sitting on your head. How do you like that, Crystal?*

"You know, in that movie." Celeste blinked and held her head at an angle. She had a way of getting the most out of her fading eyes by finding the light first, and navigating the voice's place in relation to it. If Adrienne had wanted to be particularly cruel, she could have pointed out, long ago, how it gave her the look of someone brain damaged. All Celeste needed to do was drool. But she would wait for the right time.

Instead, she said, "There's a lot of movies."

"You know. It won every award. It was made in New Zealand." Celeste bobbed her head, forward and back, like a chicken. "It had that guy in it. From *The Matrix*."

"That movie with that guy from that thing. That narrows it down for me. Who was it, fucking Keanu Reeves?"

Brooke threw her drink. It was crème de menthe, nabbed long ago from her mother's liquor cabinet. She had been sipping from a heavy mug, and it hit Adrienne square in the chest. The liquor made a spray across Adrienne's blouse, down to her lap, sticky, sickly, sweet. It was said that your remaining senses got stronger if you lost one. It was said that this was untrue, that you only grew to rely on the senses you had left. Adrienne was inclined to the latter; Brooke didn't need any shifting light. She was like a mystic or a sensei. Very likely, she could smell you from a block away. Or maybe Brooke had gotten lucky. Maybe Brooke knew as much.

But she had meant to hit Celeste.

Celeste snorted; it might have been a huge and braying laugh, had she not remembered herself.

Brooke calmed and sat. "It's not a fantasy."

Adrienne and Celeste took their places beside her, flanking her as disciples. Now was the time to be serious. Celeste asked, "Who do you think's in it?"

Adrienne pinched her thigh.

Celeste reiterated. "Who's in it? Besides Ivy Day."

vy Day had been nominated for an Oscar, a BAFTA, a Palme d'Or, a Golden Globe, a Young Artist Award, an Independent Spirit, a Fangoria Chainsaw, a Gotham, and a Golden Razzie. She had never actually won anything. There had been outrage during the previous awards season that she had come away empty-handed. She had been paired with George Clooney, Idris Elba, Brad Pitt, Jake Gyllenhaal, Michael Shannon, Barry Jenkins, Gael Garcia Bernal, F. Murray Abraham, and John Lennon. She lived alone.

There was a conflict.

If she won something, if she took up a steady man (and it had to be a man), she would secure her place in the shifting firmament. Her star would be fixed on Hollywood's Walk of Fame. She would appear in *Vogue*, discussing not Stanislavsky, but motherhood: *Ivy Day Says, "It's a Balancing Act"*. No more training into the night. No more building her up and scraping her away, going under the knife and coming at once fully-geared and camera ready. Her body would belong to her, and shouldn't she feel gratitude? Forever guaranteed a place on the shelf of the National Film Registry. And there she would remain, accessible. And there she would remain, ho hum.

Paris is Burning is in the National Film Registry, and half the queens documented went back to hooking.

Someone shat on Donald Trump's star on the Walk of Fame.

If she never took home an Oscar, if she never manacled herself to Idris Elba or Brad Pitt. She could only go up and up and up and up. Imagine that. They say the sky's the limit—very likely, Ivy Day had already punctured the stratosphere.

She had retreated to her home in New Mexico for a quick reprieve. Her legs were pinned and splinted and screwed. She could now rotate her left foot all the way around; she nearly had command of it now, though she walked lightly on it. The scars were minor, and in time and therapy and cosmetic magic, they would fade. She had had her hair shorn at the neck, colored nearly white. It echoed Jayne Mansfield or Taylor Swift, but no one would make the comparison. She still could not see out of her left eye; this was a new prosthetic, the best of its kind, as functional and as gemmed as those she had been born with. The optic nerve was grafting to this new crystal, and she was informed that she would have both eyes up and working within a week. Meantime, she made do with reading head tilted to the right.

Once upon a time, she had worn an eyepatch.

It came to her this way, *once upon a time*, because it felt like someone else's story.

But it was hers, from when she was Mary.

When she was Mary, her eye had been lazy. This part of her was a diamond refraction that had remained clear over the years, enough to make her sit down. The eyepatch had been blue. Before that, she had worn thick glasses that made her look like a Mongoloid. Had anyone laughed? She had a dim impression that no, no one had laughed; everyone had been very nice to her, as a matter of fact. It was a simpering, sticky sort of niceness, like pity. Perhaps people really had thought she was a Mongoloid. It gave grown-ups the green light to pet her head whenever they wanted or make her sit in a corner.

Now people ached to touch her. But no one did.

As if prompted, she moved from the corner armchair to the dead middle of the room, lit by the window, immersed by the sun, and then radiating her own glow against Mongoloid Mary. She creaked when she bent to sit.

The New Mexico earth ship was built on a plateau, set partway into the rocky ground, like the Bandelier settlement. It overlooked the canyon and the plunge into scrub and hard dust. The sitting room window was meant to capture the shifting sun, filling the room both day and night, bloodied at dawn and dusk. You ignored the scrub and dust, but there it was.

Nowhere to go but down.

Back to Mary and her eyepatch, obscurity, stickiness.

Ivy Day straightened her hair. She did not smile, for her smile was not something she was known for. Her natural expression was one of pink serenity, in the way of the Blessed Virgin. Not cynical, not stuck-up. It was what people liked about her.

Come unto me, all ye that labour and are heavy laden, and I will give you rest.

The ache in her eye had been steady since its implant. Now it had traveled, behind her ear to the top of her skull, until it shook her. It was horrible. She stood, opened one eye, the bad one. It was also the eye that stayed open when she winked. She had expected darkness and heightened noise. Instead, the sun, immediate. It almost blinded that eye again, though she remembered to turn her face away from the window. Before long, the room arranged itself, lines with the colors. The spots went. It was better than contact lenses.

She creaked when she stood.

Save these organs.
Save this body.
Save your servant.

The new film had a scene that involved some sort of parade. It was the climax of the picture. That was all anyone was let to know. There were confidentialities, non-disclosures, mum's-the-word. Even some of the crew was kept in the dark. Legality had plucked the pomp and circumstance from the rest of the plot and planted it in the middle of town, like divine intervention.

Here were lights, camera, flowers in action, barrels of confetti shaped like petals. Here were streamers, balloons. Here were detours to the highway, to school. People moaned of inconvenience, but could not deny the thrill—a movie, right in their own hometown! They, as locals, could point to this street and know that it was not some painted recreation on a

Hollywood backlot. This was their street. Here was the Job Lot, with the balloons forever in front. Here was the post office, the flag always at half-mast, not because of any recent tragedy, but because the rope was stuck and no one had bothered to fix it and, by now, everyone had gotten used to it. Here was where you could get the best burrito in town, the best ice cream, the best BLT, the best cappuccino.

Here was Andy. Here was Barbara. Here was Charles. Here were people you knew, people who were more than extras because they lived here. They didn't know the plot, as clueless about the movie as their own narratives. They didn't know what would happen in the next hour, in this world or the one they would go back to when the cameras turned off. That was the golden of it, real people at a parade as real people at a parade, their town as their town.

Godard wrote *Breathless* as an ode to Paris.

Nashville was Altman's love letter to Nashville.

"I wish you could see what I see," Adrienne sighed.

Celeste and Brooke strained for colors and, grasping none, wept.

JOHN MARK had meditated on it, heavily. It brought on an ache that migrated from behind his eyes to the back of his throat, bringing nausea. This symptom alone ought to have been enough to inspire doubt, if he believed in those kinds of signs. But ideas, when they struck him, had a way of clinging with many hooks; if he disengaged one, the others would hunker down all the more until he felt it feed off him, like a tick. Finally, whatever it was, a worry, a notion, would drive him to see it through. He might scour the newspapers again and again, usually the same article, to make sure that he had read it correctly, that the words had not changed, that no code lay between the letters for only the most acute reader to find.

Sometimes, you have to do the work yourself when an idea occurs.

Others, it unfolds for you. Like that.

Like that.

He was hosing the table down. A man lay upon it. JOHN MARK ought to have excused himself, for this was a fellow he knew. That was protocol: if a diener recognized the deceased, they were to have the work reassigned. But JOHN MARK could not have allowed anyone else with the fellow he knew. He'd been let to resume some of his duties, after a probation period, more janitorial than mortuary, and it had made him feel dirty and low. He could not use the plaster pump, nor could he use many of the instruments. But he could use the hose and the scissors, and he could take an inventory.

The suds spun around stiff limbs, pearled in the little hairs. The fellow on JOHN MARK's table had painted an inch thick in his last hours, more than he ever had in life. It was as though he were preparing for this moment. JOHN MARK scrubbed the foundation. Lipstick and liner ran, blood and black streaks that went into the spirals of the ears; JOHN MARK scraped it clean with a toweled finger. The fellow groaned, gases leaving the body and shaking the vocal cords. But he rounded them out into words. JOHN MARK bent to hear them: "Don't. Don't. Leave it."

"It'll run. You can't reapply it."

"Don't care. Leave it. Leave it."

"What's the point? You're not pretty anymore."

"Leave it."

"I can't."

Ivy Day's line, her face on his face, was a contrast to the inventory that JOHN MARK had taken earlier.

cargo pants, khaki, size M
denim shirt, size M
t-shirt, white, size S
Reebok sneakers, black, size 10

The fellow had not protested when JOHN MARK had cut the clothes away, drab things that could have been anybody's. Scissor in a straight line, up the chest, down the leg, like a surgery. Peel them off, pants in a pile, shirts in a bag. Shoes to the Goodwill, where JOHN MARK always got his.

From the table, a croak, *"Don't."* This time, there was an ictus on the word. If the fellow had had a full grasp on his faculties, he would have been shouting. It reminded JOHN MARK of the scene in *Gone with the Wind*, where Scarlett O'Hara sees the leg amputation of a Confederate soldier. Gangrene, they had to work fast. All out of anesthetic, and so the soldier was wide awake and screaming. *NOT MY LEG. NOT MY LEG. DON'T CUT—*It was the part that JOHN MARK had to fast-forward.

From the table, again. *"Don't."*

The rag was wet. It soaked through the inch thick. This, the fellow who had been JOHN MARK's evangelist, the one who ran the fan club out of Hooray for Hollywood, this was what he looked like. His cheeks, puffy. His eyes, small, red. His lips, gone. Skin like paste. Pocks, acne, wormy grey hairs. Not ugly. Not anything. He resembled nothing so much as a bowl of oatmeal.

The fellow sighed. The sound was oily. "Now you've done it. You took my face off."

JOHN MARK swallowed. He wanted to sit.

"You look sick," the fellow said.

"How would you know that? You can't see."

"I have an idea."

JOHN MARK did sit. "What happened?"

"Gas oven."

"Those're dangerous."

"Not many places have them anymore." It took strength for the fellow to get that much out.

JOHN MARK rubbed his forehead. Ivy Day's concealer smeared across his palm. "Sylvia Plath." There was more to that, but he didn't have any more words. He had never read any Sylvia Plath, anyway.

From the table, a liquid echo. "Sylvia Plath."

"You like Sylvia Plath?"

"She's okay."

"You wrote poetry?"

"No."

"What did you do? In life?"

A whine rose from the fellow's throat, more gases expelled. The room stunk. The fellow's voice creaked, drier now, "Nothing. Not good at anything. Nothing. But—" The air changed, the way it does the moment before someone enters a room, the moment before someone takes a step. Was the fellow going to rise? It was clear that he wanted to, though these hours had stiffened him, arms, legs and lips, words made articulate through gurgles and leftover emissions. "But. I did this." Something black puddled beneath him and dripped from the table. "Someone will get it."

It took JOHN MARK a moment to understand. And then he did. Like that.

It reminded him of a movie that Ivy Day had been in a few years back. It was called *Our Lady of the Caldera* and it was a Western. She had played a lady outlaw, known as La Sentencia, who had betrayed her band of robbers in order to secure the location of a treasure buried in a convent. At the end, the robbers escape their prison cells and track her down. By this time, she has instead taken the vows of the convent and leaves the treasure in its place. She is known now as Sister Angelica. The robbers, a bloodthirsty crew of men, give no thought to her conversion and ransack the convent. They rape the nuns, cut them dead. Before burning the convent to the ground, they prepare to have La Sentencia shot. She obliges. She sits in a chair. She folds her arms when the thugs move to tie her up. "You don't trust me?" she asks, and they leave her. The men stand abreast, one pistol each. She faces them, legs cocked, unafraid, just waiting. Her last words, before dropping: "You're not half the men your mothers are."

Lee van Cleef was called Sentenza, or The Sentence, in the Italian version of *The Good, The Bad, and The Ugly*, not Angel Eyes, as he is known in America.

Someone will get it.

It was probably why the movie did so well in the first place. There were enough *Dollars* fans to clamor for it.

There is nothing new under the sun.

If you can't make something new, you can still make something great.

"Put my face back on," the fellow croaked. In a while, maybe less, he would be completely gone. "Don't let me look this way forever."

JOHN MARK had a lipstick, Ivy Day's Valley of Roses matte. He had time before the second crew came in to fill with plaster, remove the stuff inside. With a steady hand, he traced the shape of the fellow's lips. Then he painted.

***

He never saw why Judas was given so little credit. Without Judas, where would we be? Without Judas, there would be no savior. And without a savior, there would be no absolution. And if there were no hope of absolution, he would not feel as he did.

JOHN MARK knew sacrifice. He already ate little, slept rough in a small apartment, made do with what he had. That was sacrifice as you would think of it, anyway, in its meanest form. When you were ready to abandon what other people thought of you, right now, in your lifetime, that was something. He did not have to be liked right now, in his lifetime. He did not recall having been anything other than a mean flower in a great pasture. Not to be looked at or picked, maybe stepped on. What kind of life was that? Better to be something poisonous. Better to be a Venus flytrap, something that people would recognize from a distance and say of it, "Watch out for that one."

To sacrifice your life, that was something. He couldn't argue with that. But, compared to what came with sacrificing your comfort, your good name—well, it looked much easier then, didn't it?

Playing the martyr bought you a halo. It smacked of romance, fans and disciples coming in droves to your tomb, your house, your favorite Burger King. Your truth was stretched, and everyone knew it, but no one minded. You were made greater than what you were.

Now, if you were the knife that cut. The fire. The bullet. The vile hand who took their beloved away. The one they all pointed a finger at. Everyone knew your name, too. They knew where you lived. They knew where you bought your hamburgers. They tracked you down, not to kiss, but to spit. They burdened you with insults the way they heaped their beloved with titles. You were the bastard, not the Blessed; that was the name they would ink for you in the history books. They would urinate on your doorstep. They would shatter your windows with bricks. They would send letters of hatred to your place of work, wait for you in the parking lot with a hammer, a knife, bare hands. Bare hands, maybe just that; on the bastard, it was what everyone said they would use: *If I could just get my bare hands on him...*And on your front door, they would scrawl your sobriquet: BASSTARD. They wouldn't even spell the word right, not for you.

But didn't they know, as you did, that you had to do it?

Didn't they know the burden?

As a martyr, you didn't have to stick around. Here was the bastard, bearing your responsibility, your sins, too, if you had any.

JOHN MARK had it coming to him, and he welcomed the fear. It was not unlike the anticipation of jumping headlong into a lake whose surface was thinly iced. You love the welling in your throat, so thick it is nearly solidified. Then the plunge.

n the final cut of the film, their screen time would add up to roughly thirty seconds. Their looks preceded their faces, bright lipstick and (on two of the three) big, dark glasses.

They held hands. The girl in the middle, the one who did not wear dark glasses, seemed to be the one who had the lay of the scene, the one who knew where the steps ended and the sidewalk began. The girls who flanked her absorbed the rest. One, her mouth gaping, her nose to the air; everything had an odor, as everything had a taste. The other, her head wavering between her shoulders, smooth movements, not cocking this way and that like a bird's; all sounds differed, though by now she had learned the flow of them and knew that no noise was ever truly spontaneous.

For thirty seconds, they were a single entity. They had three heads and six legs. They appropriated the world, head to head, someone blind to something, interpretation given and received.

This was the creature that came to be known as the Extras.

This was the part of the movie that people paused, rewound.

There was a rumor about this part.

Someone would say, "Stop. Stop it here."

Another would say, "You can't see anything. They would've cut this part."

Someone would reply, "They left like a millisecond in the final cut. That's why you have to pause."

In *The Wizard of Oz*, if you pause and look, you can see the outline of a Munchkin, hanging from a prop tree.

In *The Shining*, if you pause and look, you can see explicit phallic images in the carpet of Room 237.

Someone would point and say, "There. Right there."

Another would say, "Right where? The cut's too soon. You can't even tell. You don't even know."

Someone would reply, "See that? Look in the upper right, when they do the close-up on the middle girl's head. Look in the upper right corner. That little bit of black. That's the moment. That's the gunman. Then they cut to something else."

Thirty seconds amounts to a sweeping shot, taking in the wealth of people along the sidewalk of a small town, separated from the street by wooden barricades. It's a parade scene, lots of confetti, a brass band, floats overflowing with paper blooms. And atop the center float, Ivy Day, gowned, beribboned, crowned, flanked by other beauties, also crowned, beribboned, crowned.

Was it a pageant? Or a festival? A holiday or the outcome of an election? What was this movie about? Who knew. It was difficult enough for people to remember the title. Everyone had come to know this picture as "Ivy Day's last".

The sweeping shot casts over the faces of three young girls, two in dark glasses. The one in the middle, the one who does not wear dark glasses, falls forward a bit, like someone tripping over her shoelace. It's here that you can see the building behind, what looks to be a church. It is, in fact, a library, repurposed from its old incarnation as St. Paul's Church of All Saints, Episcopal. Here is where people stop the film and, if they have the technology on their TV sets, zero in on the little shape in the bell tower. It has a head, two arms, two legs. It is a moving shadow, ducking into the dark almost too quickly for the TV. But you saw it, like the hanging Munchkin, like the penises in Room 237's carpet.

"They wouldn't leave something like that in," someone always says. "You're just seeing what you want to see."

Maybe it's a trick of the light.

But does that have to leave room for doubt?

"They never reshot this part," another will point out. How someone would know this is impossible, but information, true or false, can be farmed everywhere. "They had to leave him in. That's the gunman."

"Is that the girl who died first? The one who fell over?"

"Yes, that's her."

The girl in the middle falls forward. She looks as though she had been unplugged, not so much falling as slumping. Her face droops, but that could be an illusion.

Cut to Ivy Day. She waves. She smiles. There is confetti. There are blue skies and applause, the assurance that all is well.

He got the idea from TV. Maybe the radio. It was a song, anyway.

JOHN MARK removed a linen shirt (size M) and matching trousers (size M) from a woman who had been wheeled in from her kitchen floor. She had been preparing dinner, a blood clot, shutting everything off before she had the time to feel it. The food was still on the stove when the paramedics came, pasta Bolognese. Absently, her husband had offered the ambulance team some before they went. "We made a lot," he'd said, "I won't eat it."

"He could've frozen it," the woman croaked from the table. JOHN MARK kept scissoring away her clothes. "One of them spilled sauce on the carpet. It'll stain."

She should have gone from the hospital to the designated funeral home. But through some error (clerical, divine), the hospital sent her here. Calls were made, people were coming, either from the funeral home or the family. Someone was going to collect her, anyway.

JOHN MARK wouldn't have much time with her. It wouldn't be Extreme Unction, but it was a last confession. This had to be the thing that separated the beyond from the ghosts, and JOHN MARK was beginning to understand that now. Now and then, someone he knew from the table would show up in his apartment, sometimes in the produce aisle of the HEB. Always peripheral, always gone before he could look at them full-on. Now and then, one of them would be bold enough to get close enough to whisper in his ear. They left no odor. There was nothing he could do anymore; he knew it and they knew it.

The woman knew it, too, and she made the most of her time. She had been watching something on the TV, she was saying, either about JFK or George Wallace. "Someone who got shot, anyway. I wasn't watching too closely." She was one of the most talkative ones to come to the table. JOHN MARK listened, washing her hair, draining the water and watching the suction catch at her thigh. "I was alive during both of them, though. I don't think I watched too closely then, either. When it was news. It was just another day for me. It might as well have just been TV."

JOHN MARK nodded. "Do you remember where you were?"

"What do you mean?"

"You know. When something big like that happens, people like to remember where they were."

On 9/11, JOHN MARK was in line at a Dairy Queen. What he remembered was the strangeness of eating ice cream at ten o'clock in the morning; they had let everyone out early at work, and he found himself with a craving for an Oreo Blizzard. The cashier didn't do the usual trick of turning the cup upside down to show that the Blizzard was so thick it wouldn't spill. She was watching the news.

The woman sighed, bubbling in her throat. "I don't—No—" And her voice took on a clarity and volume that was nearly audible beyond JOHN MARK's hearing. "—no. No. When Kennedy was shot. When Kennedy was shot, I was in school. I don't know how old. Maybe a freshman. I wore those tacky Weejun shoes. I had flunked a math test, and I was more upset about that than—"

On the radio, Peter Gabriel sang, *We were made for each other, me and you.*

The woman went on, rushing now because the breath left her was short, "—they let us out of school that day at noon, and I walked home. It was the first time I'd ever failed anything. You know how it is. Like the bottom has dropped out. And the pressure was on because Dad had been laid off and money had been tight enough as it was. I had to get the big scholarships if I wanted college. I couldn't get it together, in anything, it seemed. It felt like what was happening then was going to keep going on as it was, just going on and going on like that forever. Just bleak. Of course, that's silly. But you can't tell that to a kid, they don't believe you. I remember hearing what that guy had used. What was his name, Osgood—no, Oswald, that's it, Oswald. It was a 6.5x52 millimeter Carcano rifle. Not that I know what any of that means, I don't know anything about guns. Just that's what Oswald used. And it's one that my dad had. He collected, you know, he had all these antique pistols and whatever in our basement and he restored them. I don't think he ever bought ammo for any of them, they were just décor.

"But I thought," she said, "I thought that I might just go down into that basement. I might just get that Carcano. And I wouldn't have anything to worry about anymore. I'd blow my head off, and that would be it. I know, it sounds stupid now. Imagine." She wheezed. "I almost blew my head off years ago. Would've cut all this short. All because I flunked a math test."

"What was it?"

"What was what?"

"The gun. That Oswald used."

"Carcano." She was fading.

Peter Gabriel sang, *I wanna be somebody, you were like that, too.*

But then she got a second wind, all very fast, "I still have it. When Dad passed, that was my inheritance. All those guns. I never did get a license or anything. I was never into it. So, I sold most of them. I got a pretty penny. I probably could've gone on *The Antiques Roadshow* and made a mint. But I couldn't complain. What I got financed some nice things, a trip to Aruba, down payment on a new car. A Honda, but still—"

"You still have it." The woman went quiet, and for a moment, the room felt full of static. JOHN MARK snapped his fingers next to her ear. Then he hissed, knowing that it wouldn't do any good. That wasn't how it worked; she would talk when she wanted to, for as long as she wanted to. Until she was ready. Nevertheless, he tried again, "You still HAVE it."

He was shocked by his own voice. He hadn't spoken for most of his shift. Now at its ninth hour, the vibration made him jump.

The woman laughed. "What, you have a bone to pick with someone?"

"No."

"You a collector?"

"No."

"I didn't think so. You didn't seem like one. And you don't strike me as vengeful." She quieted for what amounted to a full minute. "I don't think you could hit the broad side of a barn, to be honest."

JOHN MARK was indignant. "I did archery in high school. I had a pretty good eye."

That hazy era, too far away to have been a part of his own narrative. Had he been any different from the way he was now? It seemed so. He recalled a different body, golden-skinned and wiry. He was fading. He had faded. He had told someone, a girl who was gangly but golden-skinned, too, that she was too much, and then dismissed her as nothing. Sometimes he was on top of her, his face in her neck. Her hands were across his back. Other times, he was on one knee. It didn't matter then what he did because there would be more days and more people and time would repeat itself. He would remain at his peak, a beautiful stasis. He could be someone tomorrow, or the day after, or the day after that.

His head hurt.

"Well, well." The woman on the table cackled. "William Tell."

Chatty as she was, she seemed to take her going in stride.

With some others, there was much wailing and gnashing of teeth, though this was nothing that you could see, even hear. It was more of a clarity, the way you know that someone is speaking to you with their voice or their gestures. Now that they were on the table and their faculties had left them, they were reduced to their barest energies, hovering around their old haunt like a stink. The body is all at once everything they have known and some are loathe to leave it, though in life they had been loathe to stay. JOHN MARK often thought it must be no different from being born; an infant wonders, *Why am I being made to leave this warm, dark place?,* into chill and a vacuum of light and commotion? No one wants to be born; no one wants to die.

The woman on the table sighed, made a little noise, an *Aaaahhh* of the kind you make when you get up and have a good stretch. "Didn't think I'd see this again," she said.

"What?" JOHN MARK leaned in. People on the table talked about a lot of things before they were really gone, but none had said anything of what was on the other side. "What is it?"

"You know," the woman told him, enjoying being coy.

"No, I don't."

"It's like cotton candy. That's all I'm saying."

JOHN MARK was disappointed. He'd hoped for—he didn't know what. A wormhole to the next life. Transformation. Enlightenment. He'd hated the thought of Heaven, to be honest. It smacked of anonymity. When you got to Heaven, you became one head in a unit of heads, nameless, colorless, sexless, robbed of your accumulated private creed.

He had seen what it looked like in a magazine; the article had photos of people who had sheared all their body hair and donned white robes and, peculiarly, red tennis shoes. There were twelve of them, living together on a ranch somewhere, and they called each other by a number. It had sounded like an episode of *The Prisoner. You are Number Six.*

You don't live a good life to become a eunuch.

So, he repeated, desolate, "Cotton candy."

"That's right."

"Do you see anyone?"

"No. Why would I?"

"Hear anyone?"

"Like who? Who would I be hearing?"

JOHN MARK snarled. "I don't know." The complacency itself was like cotton candy, sticky and cloying and if he listened to any more of it, he was sure he would vomit. "Your mother. Your father. Jesus. Jim Morrison. Anyone."

"Nope. Nothing like that. I wouldn't call it a noise. No people at all. And I'll be happy never to hear 'Light My Fire' ever again." She paused. "He was an asshole. Not a lot of people know that."

JOHN MARK thought that she was talking about Lee Harvey Oswald, because that was who he was thinking about. "He had his reasons, I'm sure. Why else would he have done what he did?"

But she was thinking about Jim Morrison and told JOHN MARK that he wasn't a very good listener. "He threatened to cut up an ex-girlfriend's face so that she wouldn't be pretty anymore and no one would love her. Except him. What the hell kind of reason could he have?"

JOHN MARK demurred, saying that he didn't know that about him. He was still thinking of Oswald.

"Well, he did. He was an asshole."

"She must have been beautiful."

The woman sputtered or tried to. It came out as a slow burble, fluids building up in her lungs, in her brain. Soon, she would be gone and she would leave him in anger. "What's that have to do with anything? I don't care if she was Liz Taylor."

JOHN MARK thought about that. Elizabeth Taylor had been lauded among the beauties of the world, her violet eyes, her even profile, her great and terrible romance with Richard Burton. At her peak, she had surpassed Marilyn Monroe. Liz

Taylor had lived longer than anyone had secretly anticipated, and each passing year had left another line, bloated her a little more, and you didn't see her in movies anymore. The last picture JOHN MARK had caught her in was *The Flintstones*, in which she had played Fred's bitchy mother-in-law. What kind of ending to a legacy was that? From *Cat on a Hot Tin Roof* to *The Flintstones*. Eventually, you never heard about her again, even now. When she did come up in conversation, it was in irony, old ladies who said things like, "Well, we all wanted to look like Liz Taylor. Now we do."

He couldn't think of anything else to say, save to repeat, "She must have been beautiful." He was thinking, in part, of Liz Taylor.

Why did he wear makeup, when he didn't want to be a woman?

Why did he paint his nails, when it was not out of vanity?

People asked him these things, people at work, mostly, but lately, the question had come from folks on the street, the ones from the table who showed up in his periphery.

You might ask a bhikkhu why he shaves his head.

You might ask a nun why she wears a veil.

To look like the Buddha, who began his journey to Enlightenment by living as a beggar.

To be like the angels, who cover themselves in the presence of God.

They were Angie, Becky, Crystal.

They returned to themselves in the moment before the sighted one, the one who called herself Adrienne, fell.

The one who called herself Celeste had time enough to duck.

The one who called herself Brooke had caught the knowledge of it somehow, a sound, a scent carried from its origins on the air, the wings of birds, car emission.

What did they used to look like before? Even Angie, the sighted one, didn't remember. What did she like? She hadn't had a BLT in months. She had been living off cake frosting. The last book she had read was *The Fault in Our Stars*, because everyone was reading it; she didn't remember any of it. She remembered minutes alone, in her room, in the backyard, going to school when she used to walk by herself, when she had looked forward to that walk. Then came this desperation to be with other people. Who you were became who you were seen with, what you were supposed to like. She used to be pretty good at making things out of clay. She used to be pretty good at knitting. She was the one who always won at Scrabble, even though she only ever came up with short words while everyone else struggled to spell *thermometer* or *vicarious.*

She might have thought, before she dropped, that she didn't like cake frosting at all anymore.

She might have thought that she ought to have gone blind, too, for didn't she have it coming to her as much as Becky did, as much as Celeste did?

Instead, she thought that something had bitten her. Whatever it was must have taken a bite out of her head.

Of course, she hadn't seen the gun.

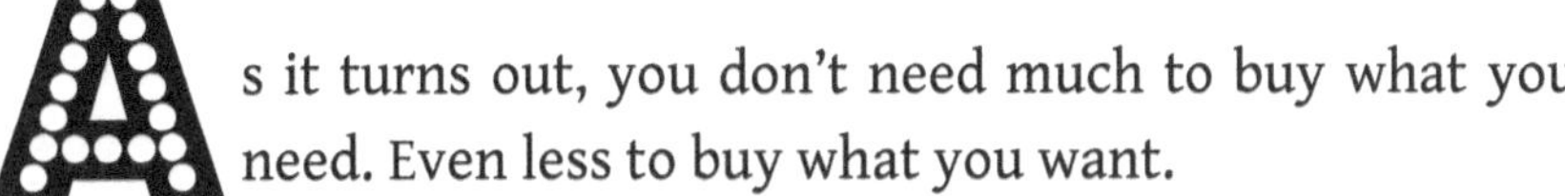

s it turns out, you don't need much to buy what you need. Even less to buy what you want.

JOHN MARK had photo identification. He had considered using a fake, for God knew, there were enough of them in the Lost and Found vaults, the name spot on and the picture a little off, or the name a little off and the picture a dead ringer. He had that kind of face and that kind of name.

But he was bold. He wanted to be seen. He had that kind of face and that kind of name, one that bursts in the collective mind for an instant, bright and terrible, and then it is gone. Andy Warhol called that your Fifteen Minutes. And shouldn't everyone be entitled to such a brief allotment? Fifteen minutes, the time it took for ads to run. But you remembered them, and bought your deodorant, your cereal, you grabbed a Big Mac.

Most people didn't have that divine aura; most realized it, or admitted it, too late. It was better to know your station, JOHN MARK knew. He had made peace with where he was long ago, a second-rate fellow, possibly third, who would go under when his ability to be employed ran out. He was a diener. His were the scraps. What would he be, when he was no longer his job?

Better to have what you could. What was it that F. Murray Abraham had said, as Antonio Salieri at the end of the film, *Amadeus? I speak for all mediocrities in the world. I am their champion. I am their patron saint.*

He had never held a firearm in his life, save for an arrow that he had lit on fire in a fit of tomfoolery and shot, bullseye.

He had been seventeen when he did that. A girl had been watching.

He did not go directly home from the morgue. The pro-shop was wedged between a Cross-Fit studio and a Jimmy John's, across the road from his apartment. Five years he had lived there, and he had never noticed it. Inside, it was small, bright lights overhead, the buzzing of electricity a constant beneath the radio, a lot of Rush, then a lot of Queen. It smelled of leather and dried meat. He was there for close to three hours, just walking, just looking, and the fellow behind the register seemed to understand, save to tell JOHN MARK that there were new cameras in every corner, there, there, there, and there, and that there had been a burglary here last month, and that you couldn't be too cautious. JOHN MARK nodded and assured the fellow behind the register that he had taken up an interest in guns. There were many in this shop, and he was ashamed to admit (to himself and to the fellow at the register) that he didn't know a derringer from a Kalashnikov, though he knew that both performed the same task when used once, correctly.

He knew that John Wilkes Booth had used a derringer, and Lincoln was gone. He knew that the Viet Cong used AK-47s, and American men came home by the dozens in boxes.

He had come, initially, with the Carcano in mind, but only vaguely.

Really, he didn't know what he wanted, what he was doing. It was not that he harbored doubts, now at the eleventh hour. He had pushed himself beyond that. It was that he simply could not conceive of himself as a man with a gun.

The fellow behind the register nodded. "Well, that's true of a lot of people." He came around from the desk, a bigger man than JOHN MARK had thought him to be. "Just think about what you want to do. Are you a hunter? Deer season again soon."

No, JOHN MARK was not a hunter.

"Protecting the home?"

That wasn't it either.

Not target practice, not a collector. What do you buy when you only need it once? It had always been a peeve of JOHN MARK's, that things weren't made to last, working maybe twice before it broke.

He did not tell the fellow this, of course. He heard himself affirm that he was something of a collector, a historian. He didn't know where the last part came from, but he felt it becoming true; here was someone who knew about the Winchester rifle, the gun that won the West. He asked the fellow if the shop carried Winchesters.

"You'd have to go to an antique place for one of those. But here—" the fellow shepherded JOHN MARK to a corner that sold EXPERT REPLICAS, as per the sign, inked in black on orange paper. The fellow took down an expert replica. "As a historian, you might appreciate this one. These were all made by guys who make movie props. So, you know they're made with top-notch accuracy. As close as they can make them. This is a Mare's Leg. You ever seen that show, *Wanted: Dead or Alive?* Steve McQueen? His signature weapon. It's fully-functional. But don't quote me on that."

One thousand dollars was the price, no registration because it was a replica and not the real thing. JOHN MARK didn't know how that worked, but it was enough for him and enough for the fellow at the pro-shop.

JOHN MARK had always wanted a signature of anything.

Bullets (replicas again, cheap metals melted down and molded) were extra.

Ivy Day saw him in the bell tower. She saw him through confetti and festoonery. Her gown was heavy, and under that, her legs, her bones, the meat of her, the steel that knitted her together. Beneath the glamour, she was rusting. It was now that the exhaustion had grown to this point, at which taking a step, saying a word, blinking once, twice, could bring her to her knees.

At last.

She was tired.

It would be a blessing. She could come down from the cross. Or, barring that, she could decide to never leave the tomb. Have the mourners come. For once, let the fans bear themselves to her; she imagined it, people bringing roses, though not before gripping thoroughly around the stem so they might leave drops of themselves at her doorstep. And yes, at her doorstep, for now the world would know where her houses were, unveiled like secreted shrines. And time would pass. Thousands would flock, then hundreds. Finally, she would be let to fade with grace. No sacrilege, no punches. She could join the ranks of Marilyn and Selena and Princess Di. Let someone else take her place on the pedestal, see how she'll like it.

She stepped down from the float. She was wearing a dress that was cheap tulle and spangles, a pageant affair. She forgot who she was embodying; there was a vague memory of a plain girl made beautiful by wholesome pride and a go-getter attitude. The prize was a scholarship, but there was supposed to be more than that. This was a character who would make a better world, by having won a pageant, by walking in a parade. Her name was Mary.

Ivy Day bet that she had never worn an eyepatch. In the script, she had worn glasses.

From the bell tower, he watched her. Everyone watched her, but his was trained. He wore her eyeshadow, a pink-gold that she could see from their great distance. She only saw the gun as shadow, tucked at his shoulder like an extension of his arm, a part of his jacket. It didn't matter what he used, she realized, only that he was there. Believe it or not, this was far from the first time that anyone had tried to kill her. A fellow had sent her a package, a Unabomber Christmas box, beribboned and brightly colored, that was intercepted by her security team. Another had preceded his act with letters; he wrote twice a day for a year, and then tracked her at Cannes, bursting onto the red carpet with a knife. He managed to grab her wrist before disappearing beneath a mountain of armed officers. She had been frightened, yes, though the night had gone on, as had the next day and the day after. Here was an indication of finality. Here was time, stopped.

The point of his eye had narrowed to a single point, and at first, she had not seen it, for it had hit like a bindi between her brows. Then, his hand trembled and the dot fell to her chest.

That was when she stepped down.

He missed.

Adrienne, or the girl Angie, fell.

People swarmed.

Brooke, or the girl Becky, was rooted to her place, for there was such an abundance of sound that she could not see one voice from another, one odor from another.

Celeste, or the girl Crystal, had the fluttering of hands, all peripheral, and it was to her like a swarm of bees that were prepping for attack just over her shoulder.

It did not take long for them to succumb. So much sensation, when you have only a little or none of one faculty, and great reliance on all your others. They grabbed, and for a moment, they had found each other's hands, before they were knocked away and another slid in its place. Someone was disgusted by them, for the girls were wet and hot and people got a look at them with their sunglasses torn away from their faces. Their eyeliner had run, their mascara had run, all streaky grime that flecked from their chins and into their hair, like a spatter of blood. Crystal's eyes, holding a little of their old mossy green, shuddered, each loose and out of time with the other. Becky's had finally paled and dried, no longer violet, no longer comparable to Elizabeth Taylor's or any other beauty, but were in that final stage of blindness in which nothing can be saved, not even the color. Now they hung heavily from the sockets, one a little protruded, better suited as marbles. When they found each other again, they knitted together, arms linked, heads down and crowns pressed, protecting themselves over the ones who wanted to stand in the way of Ivy Day and the bullet, to save her—or, in truth, to achieve their own fifteen minutes.

In the midst of this, Ivy Day continued to walk from the platform, toward the bell tower. Her dress was torn at the hem, but this created the effect of a train, the back end following her gait, embroidered with buds, festooned with leaves. She could not have said for sure, though she had imagined him, had seen him often enough in dreams. Here he was, slighter than she remembered, the boy who had given her a ring. She had accepted then, and he had spurned her. Now, if this was who she thought and hoped, here he was again, an offer anew. This union would not end in anonymity, as so many others did.

Better to go this way, out with a bang and not a whimper, than to rust.

Better to go this way than to be Mary or Johnny.

She walked with a limp, not the result of an injury; what held her together turned, quicker than she thought, to rust. She was looking for the red dot.

Never mind these organs.
Never mind this body.
Save your servant.
Please.

ACKNOWLEDGMENTS

Nate Ragolia, Jordan A. Rothacker, my husband, my parents, for reading/listening.

Tom Emerson, for movies.

> "Dying
> Is an art, like everything else.
> I do it exceptionally well.
>
> I do it so it feels like hell.
> I do it so it feels real.
> I guess you could say I've a call."
>
> - Sylvia Plath, Lady Lazarus

ABOUT THE AUTHOR

Pam Jones was born in 1989 and raised on the East Coast. She now lives in Austin, Texas with her husband. She studied creative writing at Hampshire College and is at work on her next book. She released *The Biggest Little Bird* with Black Hill Press/1888 Center, and *Andermatt County: Two Parables* with The April Gloaming. Her short fiction has appeared in The Cost of Paper and Boned: A Collection of Skeletal Fiction.

ABOUT THE PUBLISHING TEAM

Nate Ragolia was labeled as "weird" early in elementary school, and it stuck. He's a lifelong lover of science fiction, and a nerd/geek. In 2015 his first book, *There You Feel Free,* was published by 1888's Black Hill Press. He's also the author of *The Retroactivist*, published by Spaceboy Books. He founded and edits BONED, an online literary magazine, has created webcomics, and writes whenever he's not playing video games or petting dogs.

Shaunn Grulkowski has been compared to Warren Ellis and Phillip K. Dick and was once described as what a baby conceived by Kurt Vonnegut and Margaret Atwood would turn out to be. He's at least the fifth best Slavic-Latino-American sci-fi writer in the Baltimore metro area. He's the author of *Retcontinuum,* and the editor of *A Stalled Ox* and *The Goldfish,* all for 1888/Black Hill Press.